Lord Charles Neaves

Songs and Verses, Social and Scientific

Lord Charles Neaves

Songs and Verses, Social and Scientific

ISBN/EAN: 9783744767354

Printed in Europe, USA, Canada, Australia, Japan

Cover: Foto ©Andreas Hilbeck / pixelio.de

More available books at **www.hansebooks.com**

SONGS AND VERSES

SOCIAL AND SCIENTIFIC

BY

AN OLD CONTRIBUTOR TO *MAGA*

FIFTH EDITION

WILLIAM BLACKWOOD AND SONS
EDINBURGH AND LONDON
MDCCCLXXIX

PREFACE.

A GREAT proportion of these pieces were originally published in 'Blackwood's Magazine;' some appeared in the 'Scotsman' Newspaper; and the rest were written for the amusement of a Scientific Club, or of a circle of private friends. They were received at the time with some approbation; and they have since been collected mainly in the hope of preserving or reviving in the minds of those who were then pleased to approve of them a recollection of the feelings that attended their first reception.

CONTENTS.

viii *Contents.*

SONGS AND VERSES,

SOCIAL AND SCIENTIFIC.

—o—

THE ORIGIN OF SPECIES.

H AVE you heard of this question the Doctors
among,
Whether all living things from a Monad have sprung?
This has lately been said, and it now shall be sung,
Which nobody can deny.

Not one or two ages sufficed for the feat,
It required a few millions the change to complete;
But now the thing's done, and it looks rather neat,
Which nobody can deny.

A

The original Monad, our great-great-grandsire,
To little or nothing at first did aspire;
But at last to have offspring it took a desire,
        Which nobody can deny.

This Monad becoming a father or mother,
By budding or bursting, produced such another;
And shortly there followed a sister or brother,
        Which nobody can deny.

Excrescences fast were now trying to shoot;
Some put out a finger, some put out a foot;
Some set up a mouth, and some sent down a root,
        Which nobody can deny.

Some, wishing to walk, manufactured a limb;
Some rigged out a fin, with a purpose to swim;
Some opened an eye, some remained dark and dim,
        Which nobody can deny.

Some creatures grew bulky, while others were small,
As nature sent food for the few or for all;
And the weakest, we know, ever go to the wall,
        Which nobody can deny.

A deer with a neck that was longer by half
Than the rest of its family's (try not to laugh),
By stretching and stretching, became a Giraffe,
　　　　Which nobody can deny.

A very tall pig, with a very long nose,
Sends forth a proboscis quite down to his toes;
And he then by the name of an Elephant goes,
　　　　Which nobody can deny.

The four-footed beast that we now call a Whale,
Held its hind-legs so close that they grew to a tail,
Which it uses for threshing the sea like a flail,
　　　　Which nobody can deny.

Pouters, fantails, and tumblers are from the same source
The racer and hack may be traced to one Horse:
So Men were developed from monkeys, of course,
　　　　Which nobody can deny.

An Ape with a pliable thumb and big brain,
When the gift of the gab he had managed to gain,
As a Lord of Creation established his reign,
　　　　Which nobody can deny.

But I'm sadly afraid, if we do not take care,
A relapse to low life may our prospects impair;
So of beastly propensities let us beware,
    Which nobody can deny.

Their lofty position our children may lose,
And, reduced to all-fours, must then narrow their views,
Which would wholly unfit them for filling our shoes,
    Which nobody can deny.

Their vertebræ next might be taken away,
When they'd sink to an oyster, or insect, some day,
Or the pitiful part of a polypus play,
    Which nobody can deny. .

Thus losing Humanity's nature and name,
And descending through varying stages of shame,
They'd return to the Monad, from which we all came,
    Which nobody can deny.

May 1861.

5

THE MEMORY OF MONBODDO.

AN EXCELLENT NEW SONG.

Air— *The Looking-Glass.*

'TIS strange how men and things revive,
  Though laid beneath the sod, O !
I sometimes think I see alive
  Our good old friend Monboddo!
His views, when forth at first they came,
  Appeared a little odd, O !
But now we've notions much the same ;
  We're back to old Monboddo.

The rise of Man he loved to trace
  Up to the very pod, O !
And in Baboons our parent race
  Was found by old Monboddo.
Their A B C he made them speak,
  And learn their *Qui, quæ, quod*, O !
Till Hebrew, Latin, Welsh, and Greek
  They knew as well's Monboddo.

The thought that men had once had tails
 Caused many a grin full broad, O !
And why in us that feature fails,
 Was asked of old Monboddo.
He showed that sitting on the rump,
 While at our work we plod, O !
Would wear th' appendage to the stump
 As close as in Monboddo.

Alas ! the good lord little knew,
 As this strange ground he trod, O !
That others would his path pursue,
 And never name Monboddo !
Such folks should have their tails restored,
 And thereon feel the rod, O !
For having thus the fame ignored
 That's due to old Monboddo.

Though Darwin now proclaim the law,
 And spread it far abroad, O !
The man that first the secret saw
 Was honest old Monboddo.
The Architect precedence takes
 Of him that bears the hod, O !
So up and at them, Land of Cakes,
 We'll vindicate Monboddo.

The Scotchman who would grudge his praise,
　　Must be a senseless clod, O !
A MONUMENT then let us raise,
　　To honour old Monboddo.
Let some great artist sketch the plan,
　　While Rogers* gives the nod, O !
A Monkey changing to a man !
　　In memory of Monboddo.

* The Rev. promoter of the Wallace Monument.

September 1861.

THE DARWINIAN ERA OF FARMING.

AIR—*Derry Down.*

O! FARMING'S not merely an art of some skill;
It's a Science, or something more excellent still :
For the Farmer has such a command over nature,
You almost might call him a kind of Creator:

Singing down, down, down, derry down.

'Twas long ago found that a Horse and an Ass
Breed a good kind of beast for a mountainous pass ;
But since Mules were invented, it never till now
Was supposed you could breed from a Horse and a Cow:

Singing down, down, down, derry down.

But all nowadays to their lessons must look :
So the Farmer must read Mr Darwin's great book,
Who proves or asserts, and has credit from some,
That from all sorts of creatures all others may come:

Singing down, down, down, derry down.

If this theory holds, and we find the right way,
There's no end of the freaks that the Farmer may play:
Getting all sorts of products from all sorts of stocks,
He may ride on his Ram and clip wool from his Ox:

    Singing down, down, down, derry down.

He may breed you a beast mingled just half and half,
From a fortunate cross of a Pig and a Calf;
When you'll cut without trouble, so neat and so nice,
Both your ham and your veal in the very same slice:

    Singing down, down, down, derry down.

As now well established beyond any question,
Variety's good both for taste and digestion;
And a Hybrid would prove a prodigious relief,
With the fore-quarter *mutton*, the hind-quarter *beef:*

    Singing down, down, down, derry down.

You must never lose heart if your mules seldom breed,
Or if some of your mixtures at first don't succeed;
Mr Darwin himself would exhort you to wait,
As he draws his own bills at a very long date:

    Singing down, down, down, derry down.

So, perhaps, when their practical worth you explore,
There's not much in these notions we hadn't before;
For they'll scarcely come true (what a subject for
  laughter!)
Till the great day of Judgment,—or say the day After:

Singing down, down, down, derry down.

THE LEATHER BOTTÈL.

A DARWINIAN DITTY.

[*For the better understanding of this "ditty," in case it should not be self-interpreting, we prefix to it two Extracts, one from Mr Darwin's 'Descent of Man,' and the other from Dr Alleyne Nicholson's 'Introductory Text-Book of Zoology,' with a relative woodcut, borrowed from Dr Nicholson's work, in which cut, as being a family portrait of our ancestor (according to Mr Darwin), our readers cannot fail to feel a strong interest. We suggest that the word Ascidian, if not spelled Askidian, ought, at least, to be pronounced so.*]

"The most ancient progenitors in the kingdom of the Vertebrata, at which we are able to obtain an obscure glance, apparently consisted of a group of marine animals, resembling the larvæ of existing Ascidians.

"These animals probably gave rise to a group of fishes, . . .· these to the Simiadæ. The Simiadæ then branched off into two great stems, the New World and Old World monkeys; and from the latter, at a remote period, Man, the wonder and glory of the universe, proceeded. Thus we have given to man a pedigree of prodigious length, but not, it may be said, of noble quality."—*The Descent of Man, and Selection in Relation to Sex.* By Charles Darwin, M.A., F.R.S., &c.; vol. i. p. 212, 213.

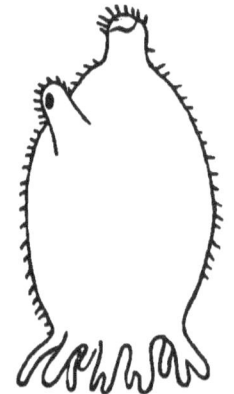

"TUNICATA.—This class includes a·class of animals not at all familiarly known, and mostly of small size. They are often called *Ascidians* (Gr. *askos*, a wine-skin), from the resemblance which many of them exhibit in shape to a two-necked jar or bottle (see fig.)—The two orifices in the outer leathery case or 'test' of the *Tunicata* lead into the interior of the animal, and are used for the admission and expulsion of sea-water; and by their means the animal both breathes and obtains food."—*Introductory Text-Book of Zoology.* By H. Alleyne Nicholson, M.D., &c.

THE LEATHER BOTTÈL.

AIR— *The Leather Bottèl.*

H OW many wondrous things there be
Of which we can't the reason see!
And this is one, I used to think,
That most men like a drop of drink.
But here comes Darwin with his plan,
And shows the true Descent of Man:
And that explains it all full well,
For man–was–once—a leather bottèl!

There are Mollusca rather small,
That Naturalists Ascidia call;
Who, being just a bag-like skin,
Subsist on water pouring in:
And these you'll find, if you will seek,
Derive their name from Heathen Greek;
For Scott and Scapula show full well
That As–kos–means—a leather bottèl.

Now Darwin proves as clear as mud,
That, endless ages ere the Flood,
The Coming Man's primeval form
Was simply an Ascidian worm:*
And having then the habit got
Of passing liquor down his throat,
He keeps it still, and shows full well
That Man–was–once—a leather bottèl.

When Bacchus' feasts came duly round,
Athenian peasants beat the ground ;
And danced and leapt to ease their toil,
'Mid leather bottles smeared with oil :
From which they slid with broad grimace,
And falling, filled with mirth the place :
And so they owned and honoured well
Their great–grand–sire—the leather bottèl.†

The toper loves to sit and swill
Of wine, or grog, or beer, his fill ;
And, as he doth but little eat,
It serves him both for drink and meat :

---

* Worm is here used for larva.   † See Virgil's Georgics, ii. 380.

But don't, I pray, be too strait-laced,
Or blame this pure Ascidian taste :
For Darwin's theory shows full well,
The to-per-is—a leather bottèl.

The Dean of Christ-Church does not shrink
To give five reasons we should drink :
" Good wine, a friend, or being dry,
Or lest we should be by-and-by : "
Then adds the fifth in humorous sport,
As " any other reason " for't :
But all his reasoning shows full well,
The Dean–was–just—a leather bottèl ! *

Nay, those who fain strong drink would stop,
Don't say, we should not drink a drop ;
But water, milk, or *eau sucrée*,
We're free to tipple all the day :
Sam Johnson's self, as you may see,
Drank many myriad cups of tea :

* Dean Aldrich's well-known Catch,
        " If all be true that I do think,
        There are five reasons we should drink,"
is a translation of the following Latin lines, which Father Sirmond, the
Jesuit, " quoique fort sobre," delighted to repeat :—
        " Si bene commemini causæ sunt quinque bibendi ;
        Hospitis adventus ; præsens sitis ; atque futura ;
        Et vini bonitas ; et quælibet altera causa."—*Menagiana*, i. 172.

And all this drinking shows full well
That man's–at–best—a leather bottèl.

"The thirsty earth drinks up the rain,"
The plants, too, drink the moistened plain :
" The sea itself, which, one would think,
Should have but little need for drink,
Drinks twice ten thousand rivers up ; "
While beasts and fishes share the cup :
The Sun, too, drinks, the Moon as well ;
So Na–ture's–all—a leather bottèl.*

I hope even Darwin don't say Nay,
When asked at times to wet his clay :
And I for one would drink his health,
And wish him sense and wit and wealth ;
And if good liquor he doth brew,
I'll drink to old Erasmus too :
And gladly join to show full well
That man–is–still—a leather bottèl.†

---

* Altered from Cowley's Anacreontics.

† Erasmus Darwin, mentioned in the last verse, was, we believe, the
grandfather of the present distinguished Naturalist. The germ of the
" Darwinian theory" is, we consider, much more certainly to be found in
the Doctor's posthumous poem of the Temple of Nature, than the origin of
man in the Ascidian larva, or leather bottèl.

THE ORIGIN OF LANGUAGE.

AN EXCELLENT NEW SONG.

AIR—*Let Schoolmasters puzzle their brains.*

'TIS not very easy to say
    How language had first a beginning,
When Adam had just left the clay,
    And Eve hadn't taken to spinning ;
Or if we suppose them to spring
    Tongue-tied from the lower creation,
What power cut their chattering string,
    Or prompted their speechification ?

    Toroddle, toroddle, toroll.

Some think men were ready inspired
    With lexicon, syntax, and grammar,
And never like children required
    At lessons to lisp and to stammer.
As Pallas by Jove was begot
    In armour all brilliantly burnished,

So Man with his Liddell and Scott
And old Lindley Murray was furnished.
Toroddle, toroddle, toroll.

Some say that the primitive tongue
Expressed but the simplest affections;
And swear that the words said or sung
Were nothing but mere Interjections.
O! O! was the signal of pain:
Ha! Ha! was the symptom of laughter;
Pooh! Pooh! was the sign of disdain,
And *Hillo!* came following after.
Toroddle, toroddle, toroll.

Some, taking a different view,
Maintain the old language was fitted
To mark out the objects we knew,
By mimicking sounds they emitted.
Bow, wow was the name for a dog:
Quack, quack was the word for a duckling:
Hunc, hunc would designate a hog,
And *wee, wee* a pig and a suckling.
Toroddle, toroddle, toroll.

Who knows if what Adam might speak
Was mono- or poly-syllabic;

Was Gothic, or Gaelic, or Greek,
    Tartàric, Chinese, or Aràbic?
It may have been Sanscrit or Zend—
    It must have been something or other;
But thus far I'll stoutly contend,—
    It wasn't the tongue of his mother.

        Toroddle, toroddle, toroll.

If asked these hard things to explain,
    I own I am wholly unable;
And hold the attempt the more vain,
    When I think of the building of Babel.
Then why should we puzzle our brains
    With Etymological clatter?
The prize wouldn't prove worth the pains,
    And the missing it isn't much matter.

        Toroddle, toroddle, toroll.

In courtship suppose you can't sing
    Your Cara, your Liebe, your Zoè,
A kiss and a sight of the ring
    Will more quickly prevail with your Chloe.
Or if you in twenty strange tongues
    Could call for a beef-steak and bottle,

A purse with less learning and lungs
  Would bring them much nearer your throttle.
    Toroddle, toroddle, toroll.

I've ranged, without drinking a drop,
  The realms of the dry Mithridates:
I've studied Grimm, Burnouf, and Bopp,
  Till patience cried "*Ohe jam satis.*"
Max Müller completed my plan,
  And, leave of the subject now taking,
As wise as when first I began,
  I end with a head that is aching.
    Toroddle, toroddle, toroll.

The speech of Old England for me;
  It serves us on every occasion!
Henceforth, like our soil, let it be
  Exempted from foreign invasion.
It answers for friendship and love,
  For all sorts of feeling and thinking;
And lastly, all doubt to remove—
  It answers for singing and drinking.
    Toroddle, toroddle, toroll.

February 1862.

GRIMM'S LAW.

*[In a late Number of the 'Anthropological Review' Grimm's law is explained in what is at least an ingenious manner. After describing an Aryan, or "articulate-speaking man," setting out to teach language to some rude owners of the "kitchen-middens" of the primeval age, who are supposed to be speechless, a distinguished Anthropologist thus reports the result of the attempt: "But now assume the 200 [kitchen-middeners] to be mutes, and follow the leader of the Aryans in his first lesson to the crowd around him. Naturally he would get the crowd to pronounce after him some short syllables, such as pa, ta, ka, to illustrate the use of lips, palate, and throat, and very naturally the four or five men (or women more likely) just in front of him would pronounce them rightly; but not one man in fifty can tell the real effect of his work on a crowd. On their returning to their wigwams, much would be the emotion of risibility and imitativeness displayed that night among the natives; and next morning the chances are that the majority who stood some distance from the speaker would have fixed for ever upon the whole nation the wrong utterance of ba, da, ga. The main point of my whole argument is, that such a result would most naturally follow among mutes, but would never happen among speaking men."—*Extract from Paper read before the Anthropological Society by the Rev. D. I. HEATH, M.A.—'Anthropological Review,' April 1867.]

GRIMM'S LAW.

A NEW SONG.

AIR—*Old Homer,—but with him what have we to do?*

ETYMOLOGY once was a wild kind of thing,
Which from any one word any other could
bring:
Of the consonants then the effect was thought small,
And the vowels—the vowels were nothing at all.

Down a down, down, &c.

But that state of matters completely is changed,
And the old school of scholars now feels quite estranged :
For 'tis clear that whenever we open our jaw,
Every sound that we utter comes under some Law.

Now one of these laws has been named after Grimm,
For the Germans declare it was found out by him :
But their rivals the Danes take the Germans to task,
And proclaim as its finder the great Rasmus Rask.

Be this as it may, few have sought to explain
How it came that this law could its influence gain:
Max Müller has tried, and, perhaps, pretty well;
But I don't understand him, and therefore can't tell.

Anthropologists say, after Man had his birth,
There were two human races possessing the earth;
One gifted and graced with articulate speech,
And another that only could gabble and screech.

The Aryans could speak, and could build, and could
    plough,
And knew most of the arts we are practising now;
But the Dumbies that dwelt at those vile Kitchen-
    Middens
Weren't fit but to do their Superiors' biddings.

So an Aryan went forth to enlighten these others,
And to raise them by speech to the level of brothers;
On the Mutes of the Middens he burst with eclàt,
And attempted to teach them the syllable PA.

This PA was intended to set things a-going
For a lot of Good Words very well worth the knowing;
Such as Pater, and πολις, and Panis, and Pasco;
But the Midden performers made rather a *fiasco.*

Scarce one of them all would say PA for a wonder,
But each blundered away with a different blunder:
Some feebly cried A, and some, crow-like, said KA,
While the nearest they came to was FA or was BA.

Then the Aryan propounded the syllable TA,
Which his pupils corrupted to THA and to DA:
Even KA, when they tried it, they never came nearer
Than to HA or to GA, or to something still queerer.

So slow were their senses to seize what was said,
That they never could hit the right nail on the head;
And the game of cross purposes lasted so long,
That it soon was a rule they should always go wrong.

Thus the Dumbies for ever said Father for Pater,
And Bearing and Brother for Ferens and Frater:
The Aryan cried Pecu, the Midden-man Fee,
In which Doctors and Lawyers to this day agree.

Jove's Tonitru sank into Old Saxon Thunner,
Which the High-German dunderheads changed into
    Donner;
From Domo came Tame, and from Domus came Tim-
    mer,
While the hissing Helvetians said Zämen and Zimmer.

From θυρα came Door, and from θυγατηρ Dochter,
Which dwindled away into Türe and Tochter;
From Hortus and Hostis came Garden and Guest,
And from χολη came Gall, which so bothers the best.

The Old Aryan GAU was the Kitchener's Koo
(Though some tribes were contented to call the beast
    Boo):
If your wife in her καρδια would give you a Cornu,
The Midden-man said, " In her Heart she would Horn
    you."

Such a roundabout race I can only compare
To the whirligig engines we mount at a fair;
Where each rides as in fear lest his steed be forsaken,
But he ne'er overtakes, and is ne'er overtaken.

A theory seldom is free from a flaw,
But the story I've told may account for Grimm's law:
Though some others suggest, if the Bible's no fable,
That Grimm's law was what caused the confusion at
    Babel.
                    Down a down, down, &c.

December 1867.

THE THREE R'S.*

YOU must own, Mrs Bull, that your family's large,
    Say, some two or three millions at least ;
And so many small children must prove a great charge,
    Which of late has been strangely increased.
To their schooling, of course, we must carefully see,
    Or a slur on us both it will fling :
But, as all of the lot cannot gentlefolks be,
    Why, I think, the three R's is the thing.

One lad must be keeping the cow from the corn,
    Or must wait on the wandering sheep :
Another must double Cape Wrath or Cape Horn—
    A cabin-boy far on the deep.
As soon as the plumes on their pinions grow strong,
    From the nest they are sure to take wing ;
So their time with the schoolmaster cannot be long,
    And 'tis clear the three R's is the thing.

* There is no intention here to advocate generally a low rate of educa-
tion. But it seems doubtful if general *compulsion* is allowable, or is likely
to be allowed, except for essentials.

To read well their Bible, to write to a friend,
  And to cast up a common account,—
This is easily taught, and though this were the end,
  'Tis a boon of no slender amount.
Would they learn Mathematics, or Grammar, or
    Greek,
  E'en supposing we gave them their swing?
Or would these make them fitter a service to seek?
  No, no; the three R's is the thing.

Would you deck out a daughter in satin and silk,
  Who must work for the bread she's to eat?
Would you send out your maids to the cow-house to
    milk,
  With fine kid-leather shoes on their feet?
Should your ploughboys, like folks at the playhouse, be
    dressed,
  As if only to dance and to sing?
No! such tawdry attire would but make them a jest:
  So again, the three R's is the thing.

Then, my dear, there's a matter I've lately observed,
  Makes me sorely our system distrust:
'Tis that some boys are stuffed, while the others are
    starved,
  Which is cruel as well as unjust.

To the general mass, to the average class,
   We should knowledge and nourishment bring:
Give them plain wholesome fare, but let each have a
   share;
   And for *that* the three R's is the thing.

1862.

28

DON'T FORGET THE RICH.

A SUPPLEMENT TO "THE THREE R'S."

"WE'LL educate the Poor," you say ; and clearly
it is right
To try to lead our humble friends from darkness into
light :
To help their hands, to fill their hearts with feelings
just and true,
To make them skilled in handicrafts, and wise and
happy too ;
Yet take with me a wider range, and seek a higher pitch,
And while you educate the Poor, pray, don't forget the
Rich.

The Poor are to be pitied much, of food and clothing
scant ;
Yet there's a kind of schooling, too, in poverty and
want.
They learn to use their eyes and ears, they can't be idle
quite ;
They must be up and doing, let the thing be wrong or
right.

But when no motive stirs the mind, there comes a serious hitch ;
For laziness and luxury are open to the Rich.

The rich man's son, I therefore think, may claim our
pity too :
He finds no want unsatisfied, he sees no work to do.
His bed is made : he's softly laid : and when he lists to
rise,
Pleasure invites and Flattery's voice its Siren magic
plies :
Strange power have these confederate foes men's spirits
to bewitch ;
So while we don't neglect the Poor, we'll also mind the
Rich.

The rich man's daughter often, too, may mourn a hap-
less fate,
If head and heart ne'er learned the art to dignify her
state ;
If life without a task or sphere is miserably spent
In languor or in levity or peevish discontent :
Scarce sadder lot has Hood's poor girl, condemned to
sew and stitch,
Than hers the unidea'd maid, the daughter of the Rich.

The untaught Poor are dangerous, they know not what
    they need :
By clamour or pernicious threats they seek their cause
    to speed :
They quarrel with their truest friends; and look with
    envious glare
On those whose industry and thrift have made them
    what they are.
But all the Blind, of guides bereft, may fall into the
    ditch ;
So give true insight to us all, the Poor as well as Rich.

What citizen can well be worse than one with wealth to
    spend,
Who neither has the power nor will to serve a noble
    end ?
Trained in his body he may be, and taught to race and
    game,
But ignorant of letters and untouched by virtue's
    flame :
Corrupted, nay corrupting too, — it little matters
    which—
Oh, if the vicious Poor are bad, what are the vicious
    Rich?

If you possess compulsion's power, compel us all to
  learn
How we may best the Good and Bad, the Fair and
  Foul discern :
Let God's great laws, let Britain's weal, be rightly under-
  stood ;
Show us the gain of growing wise, the joy of doing
  good :
Give in the social edifice to each his proper niche,
And teach their duties and their rights alike to Poor
  and Rich.

In hopes our social ills to cure, our ancient Kings and
  Laws
Built schools and founded colleges to prosper the good
  cause.
There all who came were kindly lured, or led by firm
  control,
To learn whate'er would form the mind or purify the
  soul.
These wise foundations seek to aid and elevate their
  pitch:
You'll benefit both Rich and Poor—by training well the
  Rich.

O WHY SHOULD A WOMAN NOT GET A DEGREE?

ON FEMALE GRADUATION AND LADIES' LECTURES.

AIR—Argyll is my name.

YE fusty old fogies, Professors by name,
 A deed you've been doing of sorrow and shame :
Though placed in your Chairs to spread knowledge
   abroad,
Against half of mankind you would shut up the road :
College honours and lore from the Fair you withdraw,
By enforcing against them a strict Salic law :
Is it fear? is it envy? or what can it be?
And why should a woman not get a degree?

How ungrateful of You, whose best efforts depend
On the aid certain Ladies in secret may send :
CLIO *here* writes a lecture, URANIA *there*,
And more Muses than one prompt the Musical Chair.
CALLIOPE sheds o'er the Classics delight,
And the lawyers have meetings with THEMIS by night ;

Yet, if VENUS de' Medici came, even She
Could among her own Medici get no degree.

In Logic a woman may seldom excel;
But in Rhetoric always she bears off the bell.
Fair PORTIA will show woman's talent for law,   '
When in old Shylock's bond she could prove such a flaw.
She would blunder in Physic no worse than the rest,
She could leave things to Nature as well as the best;
She could feel at your wrist, she could finger your fee;
Then why should a woman not get a degree?

Your Lectures for Ladies some fruit may produce;
For a Course of good lectures is always of use.
On a married Professor your choice should alight,
Who may lecture by day—as he's lectured at night.
And allow me to ask, what would Husbands become,
If they weren't well lectured by women at home?
When from faults and from follies men thus are kept free,
There surely the woman deserves a degree.

Yet without a degree see how well the Sex knows
How to bind up our wounds and to lighten our woes!
They need *no* Doctor's gown their fair limbs to enwrap,
They need ne'er hide their locks in a Graduate's cap.

C

So I wonder a woman, the Mistress of Hearts,
Would descend to aspire to be Master of Arts:
A Ministering Angel in Woman we see,
And an Angel need covet no other Degree.

THE READING OF GREEK.

A SONG FOR A HELLENIC CLUB.

AIR—*Lillibulero.*

T HIS life is a medley of good and of ill,
A strange alternation of joy and of grief;
Its maladies baffle both potion and pill,
Yet I've found out a cure that will give us relief.
Its aid if you borrow,
'Twill banish your sorrow,
And brighten your path when the prospect is bleak;
In short, it will be a
Complete panacea—
And it simply consists in the Reading of Greek.

The worst of our evils spring out of the mind—
We're proud and resentful, we're sordid and vain;
Take a course of my medicine, and quickly you'll find
Of every such ailment you'll cease to complain.
A winter and summer
Of Plato and Homer

Will make you quite strong where at present you're weak.
  With you or your daughters,
  The Kissingen waters
Might well be exchanged for the Reading of Greek.

If rage and revenge are the bane of your life,
  In the wrath of Achilles a beacon you'll see;
If you'd be a good husband and cherish your wife,
  Ulysses and Hector your models may be.
    The foul-mouthed Thersites
    So brimful of spite is
That nobody here to be like him would seek;
    While the beautiful Helen
    A story is telling
That reads us a lesson in Reading our Greek.

The truths that old Homer so gloriously sung,
  The spirit of Plato as nobly has said;
The sweets of Hymettus distil from his tongue,
  And a half-divine halo encircles his head.
    Of love and of beauty,
    Of drinking and duty,
He makes his own Socrates worthily speak;
    The famous old codger,
    A regular dodger,
Will teach you some tricks in your Reading of Greek.

What follies some wise-looking people commit,
  Whose fault is a thickness of blood or of skull !
Impervious to laughter and proof against wit,
  Their dreary existence flows ditch-like and dull.
    Now there's nothing on earth, sir,
    Conduces to mirth, sir,
Like the Old Comic vein of fun, frolic, and freak;
    And although to our cost, sir,
    Margites is lost, sir,
Aristophanes lives for our Reading in Greek.

Then see how around us there everywhere reigns
  A shopkeeping spirit so keen and intense,
That nobody's valued except for his gains,
  And all things are weighed by pounds, shillings, and
    pence !
    With a view to abate, sir,
    A nuisance so great, sir,
And Parliament purge of the huckstering clique,
    I'd make every new Member,
    Each month of November,
Pass through Donaldson's* hands for the Reading of
  Greek.

---

* Dr Donaldson, at one time an Examiner for the University, now Rector
of the High School of Edinburgh.

To you, my fair friends, let me now recommend
  The charming example of Lady Jane Grey:
To the good of both sexes such conduct would tend,
  For lovers will follow where you lead the way.
      In the gaily-filled ball-room,
      Or pleasanter small room,
The blush would be brought to the dandy's pale cheek,
      If his partner would try him
      With Paris and Priam,
And hackle him well on the Reading of Greek.

What a blest Revolution we then should behold,
  When true Wisdom and Wit had enlivened us all!
When the Good and the Fair should their treasures
      unfold,
  And the three-volume Novel should go to the Wall.
      But don't overdo it;
      Bring Common-sense to it:
No pedants in petticoats here I'd bespeak:
      But let household employments,
      And social enjoyments,
Alternate bear sway with the Reading of Greek.

AD SODALITATIS HELLENICÆ SOCIOS,

CARMEN

MELODIÆ APTATUM SCOTICÆ,

Cui titulus—*O'er the Muir among the Heather*.

CELEBREMUS, O! sodales,
Noctes has conviviales:
Vel legendo, vel bibendo,
Non invenietis tales.

Libri Græci hic volvuntur:
Fratres legunt et loquuntur:
Ridet jocus; adest coquus;
Et liquores consumuntur.

Ut perfecta sit doctrina,
Magnam opem fert culina:
Is qui sapit cœnam capit,
Et prudenter sumit vina.

Hæ sunt epulæ divinæ,
Ala, pectus, crus,—gallinæ :
Fricta frusta, blanda crusta,
Ostreæque submarinæ.

Interim invadit sitis,
Quæ levatur fructu vitis,
Vel Hispano, vel Germano,
Dum sit fortis et sit mitis.

At quum dapes sunt finitæ,
Gutta parva aquæ vitæ
Dat calorem, dat vigorem,
Saltem si sit mixta ritè.

Hæ dum voluptates placent,
Carmina non spreta jacent :
Sic impleti, sumus læti,
Et Camænæ raro tacent.

Quum receptum jam sit satis
Vini, cibi, græcitatis,
His pro donis, O ! quam bonis,
Gratias agamus Fatis.

Quisque tunc ad suum tectum
Abeat, et petat lectum ;
Ut profundo et jucundo
Corpus somno sit refectum.

Magnum denique clamorem,
Hujus cœtûs in honorem,
Excitemus, et laudemus
Clarum ejus Fundatorem.

NOTE.—*Convivales*, it is believed, would be a better word in the second line than *conviviales*, if it would only sing and sound as well. But the Latinity of the song throughout is not meant to be warranted as rising above that standard which goes by the name of Canine.

THE PROPOSAL OF POLTYS.

Πόλτυς, ὁ Θρᾳκῶν Βασιλεὺς, ἐν τῷ Τρωϊκῷ πολέμῳ, πρεσβευσαμένων πρὸς αὐτὸν ἅμα τῶν Τρώων καὶ τῶν Ἀχαιῶν, ἐκέλευσε τὸν Ἀλέξανδρον, ἀποδόντα τὴν Ἑλένην, δύο παρ' αυτοῦ λαβεῖν καλὰς γυναῖκας.

—PLUTARCHI *Apophthegmata.**

AIR—*O! London is a fine town.*

O!
POLTYS was a man of peace, and loved a
quiet life;
His neighbours, too, he tried to keep from bloodshed
and from strife.
He flourished in the famous times that saw the Trojan
war,
But held aloof from war's alarms, and viewed the fight
afar.

The Trojans, and the Grecians too, by every art did
try
To win o'er Poltys to their side, and make him an ally:

* See also Prior's ' Alma.'

For Poltys was a king of Thrace, and lived betwixt the
two,
And embassies arrived to him with every wind that
blew.

But Poltys said: "The case is this, that Paris, that
young scamp,
Has wheedled Menelaus' wife, and got her to decamp:
And Menelaus wants her back, though I would not do
so,   .
For when a wife resolves to run, I'd always let her go.

"Yet I've a plan by which, I think, much mischief may
be saved,
For I've two comely Wives to spare, extremely well-
behaved.
These dames on Paris I'll bestow, if Helen he'll release;
Then all of you, and Poltys too, may live and die in
peace."

This course, no doubt, if followed out, had saved much
grief and wrong;
But Homer would have wanted then the subject of his
song.

He never would have Hector known, or heard ot
  Andro-màchè,*
Would ne'er have been *traduced* by Pope, or *overset* by
  Blackie.

And then if Homer had not sung, we might have had
  no Greek,
And Plato and the Stagyrite would still have been to
  seek.
A poet Virgil ne'er had been but for his predecessors,
And where should we, or Oxford, be, without our Greek
  Professors?

Then though so many heroes fell upon the Trojan plain,
The Iliad and the Odyssey have made the loss a gain;
And that old Maxim may be true, by some so stoutly
  pressed,
That on the whole, and in the end, WHATEVER IS IS
  BEST.

* See Swift.

45

THE PENNY OF PASES.

Pasetis semiobolus.—Ex Erasmi Adagiis.
Tradunt Pasetem quendam præstigiarum et magiæ peritiâ primum nomen meruisse.—Emebat autem frequenter, pretiumque rei numerabat : verum mox nummus, non apud venditorem, sed apud Pasetem, reperiebatur.—Sic etiam apud Suidam vo. *Pases.*

AIR—*Abraham Newland.*

WHAT ills we endure
    When condemned to be poor,
Doesn't need to be told in fine phrases;
    Nor how matters would mend
    Were a Fairy our friend,
Who would give us the Penny of Pases.
    O ! for the Penny of Pases !
    The miraculous Penny of Pases !
        When he paid it away,
        Ere a word you could say,
It was back in the pocket of Pases.

It is certain that many
By turning a penny
Get wealth that all people amazes :
And so We might grow rich,
To a wonderful pitch,
Just by turning the Penny of Pases.
The astonishing Penny of Pases !
I can never enough sing its praises ;
No figures could count
The prodigious amount
We might raise by the Penny of Pases.

But I wouldn't as yet
Pay the National Debt,
Which I think one of Stuart Mill's crazes ;
Nor in luxury wallow,
And guzzle and swallow
All I got from the Penny of Pases.
When I think of the Penny of Pases,
My breast with benevolence blazes :
Such good I would do,
Such fine projects pursue,
When possessed of the Penny of Pases.

Men of wit and of worth,
The true salt of the earth,
Then should ride in their coaches and chaises ;

All moneyless merit
Should freely inherit
A share of my Penny of Pases.
With the help of the Penny of Pases,
The beef of yon bullock that grazes
    Should soon fatten all those
    Who walk loose in their clo'es
For want of the Penny of Pases.

    I would lavish my dollars
    On Poets and Scholars ;
I'd put Art on a liberal basis :
    Scientific Inventors
    Should hold some debentures
To be paid from my Penny of Pases.
The Church, too, should profit by Pases
(If it shun all Papistical phases):
    Poor Curates with charges
    Should taste of my largess,
Enriched by the Penny of Pases.

    I would portion young girls
    Who would keep their own curls,
And who wouldn't wear chignons or jaseys ;
    And, in spite of their dads,
    I would teach little lads
Some things well worth the Penny of Pases.

If I had but the Penny of Pases,
I would strew life's hard pathway with daisies:
    The Saturnian reign
    Should be brought back again,
By the help of the Penny of Pases.

    But a voice seems to ask,
    "Are You fit for this task?"
And a delicate question it raises;
    For I freely confess
    One might make a sad mess,
Misapplying the Penny of Pases.
If we look at life's intricate mazes,
Perhaps he who piously gazes
    May a Providence see
    That is wiser than We,
And that needs not the Penny of Pases.

PLATONIC PARADOXES.

A NEW SONG.

AIR— *The tight little Island.*

I N how many strange ways
    Human nature displays
The caprices that enter her pate, O !
    To which view you'll be led
    If some pages you've read
In the Oxford translation of Plato.
What a wonderful writer is Plato !
And how well Jowett's pen can translate, O !
    But I clearly discover
    On reading him over
Some very odd notions in Plato.

    The fears of the brave
    Make us always look grave,
And the mean little tricks of the great, O !

D

So the foolish things too
That the wise say and do
Are ridiculous even in Plato.
Upon some points I quite go with Plato,
In the same way as Addison's Cato :
But some marvellous flaws
As to justice and laws
Mark the model Republic of Plato.

Every honest man grieves
At the number of thieves
That our social temptations create, O !
And our hearts are all sore
For the wretchedly poor ;
And I'm sure the same feelings had Plato.
But the system propounded by Plato,
These deplorable ills to abate, O !
Was to break off with Mammon,
Have all things in common :
" Private property's gammon "—said Plato.

There can never be theft
When no property's left
To give Meum and Tuum their weight, O !
And when all's a dead level,
Starvation and revel
Alike are excluded by Plato.

These Communist doctrines of Plato
Have again come in fashion of late, O !
    But the makers of money,
    The hoarders of honey,
Won't be pleased with these projects of Plato.

    Then the struggles and strife
    Which attend married life,
And oft turn early love into hate, O !
    Its profligate courses,
    Desertions, Divorces,
Must have hurt the fine feelings of Plato.
But a very bad cure proposed Plato
(For I don't think him here *the potato*),
    " Make the man and the woman,
    Like property, *common ;*—
And the children as well : " added Plato.

    No folks were to wed
    That were not thorough-bred,
And each wedding should last a short date, O !
    And if children appeared
    Not quite fit to be reared,
They were never acknowledged by Plato.

'Twas a delicate question with Plato,
Upon which he dislikes to dilate, O !
    But we all of us know
    Where the puppy-dogs go
When the litter's too many for Plato.

    On this question that vexes
    Us as to the sexes,
Our author don't long hesitate, O !
    Women's duties and rights,
    Whether beauties or frights,
Are completely conceded by Plato.
But the pace here adopted by Plato
Seems to move at too rapid a rate, O !
    All must go to the wars
    And be servants of Mars,
Both the women and men, under Plato.

    On another small point
    He appears out of joint,
Though perhaps it admits of debate, O !
    Shall philosophers solely
    Rule over us wholly,
Or our kings be the pupils of Plato ?

Suppose them as clever as Plato,
How would Darwin or Mill rule the state, O !
Should you think Epicurus
A good Palinurus,
Or would England be governed by Plato?

A philosopher's schemes
Are made up of fond dreams
And of idle Utopian prate, O !
For while Theory preaches,
'Tis Practice that teaches,
And corrects the wild crotchets of Plato.
So the model Republic of Plato
Must submit to the general fate, O !
Lay the book on the shelf,
And each man make HIMSELF
What a Christian would wish for in Plato.

.

NOTE.—While we thus venture, under the allowed garb of ridicule, to
record some plain truths as to certain extravagant views suggested by Plato
in his Republic, we should do injustice to our own feelings if we did not at
the same time express the pleasure and admiration which have been excited
in us by the remarkable Translation of that author that has just issued
from the Clarendon Press. This work by Professor Jowett is one of the
most splendid and valuable gifts to Literature and Philosophy that have
for a long time been offered. Its first or most obvious excellence is the
perfect ease and grace of the translation, which is thoroughly English, and
yet entirely exempt from any phrase or feature at variance with the Hel-

lenic character. Very few translations, other than the Bible, read like an original: but this is one of them. It has other and more recondite excellences. It is the work, almost the life-labour, we believe, of a profound scholar, a thoughtful moralist and metaphysician, and a most successful instructor of youth : and it is manifest that the complete success that has attended his execution of the task is itself the means of concealing the diligence, industry, and ability with which philological and interpretative difficulties must have been solved or overcome. It is a great matter, even for the best scholars, to possess such a guide and help in the study of the original; and to others, desirous of knowing thoroughly and appreciating worthily the wise thoughts and literary beauties of one of the greatest writers that ever lived, the boon is inestimable.

STUART MILL ON MIND AND MATTER.*

A NEW SONG.

AIR—*Roy's Wife of Aldivalloch.*

Stuart Mill, on Mind and Matter,
All our old Beliefs would scatter :
Stuart Mill exerts his skill
To make an end of Mind and Matter.

THE self-same tale I've surely heard,
Employed before, our faith to batter:
Has David Hume again appeared,
To run a-muck at Mind and Matter?

---

* "Matter, then, may be defined a Permanent Possibility of Sensation."
—*Mill's Examination of Hamilton*, p. 198.
"The belief I entertain that my mind exists, when it is not feeling, nor thinking, nor conscious of its own existence, resolves itself into the belief of a Permanent Possibility of these states." "The Permanent Possibility of feeling, which forms my notion of Myself."—*Ibid.*, p. 205, 206.

David Hume could Mind and Matter
Ruthlessly assault and batter:
　Those who Hume would now exhume
Must mean to end both Mind and Matter.

Now Mind, now Matter, to destroy,
　Was oft proposed, at least the latter:
But David was the daring boy
　Who fairly floored *both* Mind and Matter.

David Hume, both Mind and Matter,
While he lived, would boldly batter:
　Hume by Will bequeathed to Mill
His favourite feud with Mind and Matter.

We think we see the Things that be;
　But Truth is coy, we can't get at her;
For what we spy is all my eye,
　And isn't really Mind or Matter.

Hume and Mill on Mind and Matter
Swear that others merely smatter:
　Sense reveals that Something feels,
But tells no tale of Mind or Matter.

Against a stone you strike your toe ;
  You feel 'tis sore, it makes a clatter :
But what you feel is all you know
  Of toe, or stone, or Mind, or Matter.

    Mill and Hume of Mind and Matter
    Wouldn't leave a rag or tatter :
      What although we feel the blow ?
      That doesn't show there's Mind or Matter.

We meet and mix with other men ;
  With women, too, who sweetly chatter :
But mayn't we here be duped again,
  And take our thoughts for Mind and Matter?

    Sights and sounds like Mind and Matter,
    Fairy forms that seem to chatter,
      Are but gleams in Fancy's dreams
      Of Men and Women, Mind and Matter.

Successive feelings on us seize
  (As thick as falling hailstones patter) :
The Chance of some return of these,
  Is all we mean by Mind or Matter.

Those who talk of Mind and Matter
Just a senseless jargon patter :
*   What are We, or you, or he ?—*
Dissolving views, not Mind or Matter.

We're but a train of visions vain,
    Of thoughts that cheat, and hopes that flatter :
This hour's our own, the past is flown ;
    The rest unknown, like Mind and Matter.

Then farewell to Mind and Matter :
To the winds at once we scatter
*   Time and Place, and Form and Space,*
And Heaven and Earth, and Mind and Matter.

We banish hence Reid's Common Sense ;
    We laugh at Dugald Stewart's blatter ;
Sir William, too, and Mansel's crew,
    We've done for you, and Mind and Matter.

Speak no more of Mind and Matter :
Mill with mud may else bespatter
*   All your schools of silly fools,*
That dare believe in Mind or Matter.

But had I skill, like Stuart Mill,
His own position I could shatter :
The weight of Mill, I count as Nil—
If Mill has neither Mind nor Matter.

Mill, when minus *Mind and Matter,*
Though he make a kind of clatter,
Must himself just mount the shelf,
And there be laid with Mind and Matter.

I'd push my logic further still
(Though thus I seemed as mad's a hatter):
I'd prove there's no such man as Mill,—
If Mill disproves both Mind and Matter.

If there's neither Mind nor Matter,
Mill's existence, too, we shatter :
If you still believe in Mill,
Believe as well in Mind and Matter.

February 1866.

THE IN-OSCULATION OF SCIENCE AND ART.

A LYRICAL LECTURE.*

YE linguists, pray, what does *inosculate* mean ?
　　That it's something like *kissing* a tyro can see :
But in case any ladies should come on the scene,
　　From such fervid ideas we'll try to keep free.
Let Platonic emotions, then, reign in the heart
At the In-osculation of Science and Art.

This In-osculation, of which I shall speak,
　　With In-oculation has nothing to do :
It is used, like another long compound in Greek,†
　　When our vessels join mouths, and make one out of
　　　two.
So of some recent views I'll repeat you a part
On the In-osculation of Science and Art.

---

　* Suggested by Dr Lyon Playfair's excellent Lecture on this subject at
Birmingham.
　† αναστομωσις.

What a poor helpless being is Man at his birth !
  (How unlike what we make him when trained in our
    Schools !)
Like a sailor just shipwrecked he lies on the earth,
  Without cover or clothes, without weapons or tools :
This, in Primitive Man, seems a very bad start
For the In-osculation of Science and Art.

But a Mind is within him, that sits on the watch,
  To observe and infer, to grow skilful and wise ;
And from every event some advantage to snatch,
  Till from Bad up to Better his faculties rise :
Or till Genius awakens, bright thoughts to impart
On the In-osculation of Science and Art.

Chance hits upon Fire ; and the wonderful gift
  Soon sets men on boiling or baking their food ;
And when winter comes round with his ice and his
    drift,
  We're preserved by the warmth from his surliest
    mood.
Then the Potter bakes clay, and the Smith, strong and
    swart,
Shows an In-osculation of Science and Art.

Before Father Bacchus and Ceres were known,
  Our life must indeed have been barren and bare:
To be fed upon Acorns and Water alone,
  Though the Acorns be roasted, is very poor fare:
The addition of Bread and of Wine to our *carte*
Was a mighty improvement in Science and Art.

With implements awkward Man turned up the soil,
  Till a well-fashioned plough, came his labour to
    save;
Or if doomed on the deep for subsistence to toil,
  A clumsy canoe bore him over the wave.
For 'tis long ere the Ship, with her Compass and
    Chart,·
Proves the In-osculation of Science and Art.

But onward we move in our destined career,
  The workman still working, and watched by the
    Sage;
Till the Sage, like a pilot, comes forward to steer,
  By the light shed from Nature's and History's
    page.
Then when Knowledge and Skill keep no longer
    apart,
We discover new regions in Science and Art.

Yet for how many ages had Air been respired,
  Ere its gases in part were by Priestley disclosed !
And how long had old Thales from business retired,*
  Ere the Man came who told us how Water's com-
    posed ! †
Such delays and obstructions seem often to thwart
The full In-osculation of Science and Art.

'Tis but now we find out that the Sun is the Source
  And the Centre of most of the movements we see :
His radiance gives birth to each varying Force,
  And not Proteus himself could more versatile be.
With his beams all our Energies come or depart:
All the Energies even of Science and Art.

He sucks up in mists from the wide-surging brine,
  The streams that our mountains send down to the
    plains ;
And his rays, bottled up in the deeply sunk mine,
  Are emerging to drive our swift iron-way trains.
While the herbs which he rears go to furnish the Mart
With good beeves for the lovers of Science and Art.

* It was the doctrine of Thales that the beginning of all things was Water.
† Cavendish or Watt?

Success then to Science ! success to the Sun !
 May they long to our labours their influence lend !
Their beneficent course as they gloriously run,
  May each Muse, grave or gay, on their progress
   attend :
While the Wine-cup, at times, shall its brilliancy dart
On the In-osculation of Science and Art.   .

DUST AND DISEASE.

OF the wonderful things that lie round us con-
cealed,
How much have the true Sons of Science revealed!
Good Faraday long was the foremost of these,
And now Tyndall has told us of Dust and Disease.

If a long beam of light crosses through a dark room,
It seems peopled with motes that shine bright in the
gloom :
But the gay dancing things, that the gazer thus sees,
Are in fact nothing better than Dust and Disease.

Around us, above us, on all sides they float :
They light on our skin, and they slide down our throat :
Though we don't feel or see them, yet go where we
please,
The atmosphere's laden with Dust and Disease.

E

All the varying ills to which flesh is an heir,
All the foes of both body and mind may be there.
Lusts and Fevers that burn, Fears and Agues that
    freeze,
May be mixed in these atoms of Dust and Disease.

All places alike these intruders infest,
And 'tis thought that St Stephen's is none of the best:
Where Faction and Folly are busy as bees,
There will always be plenty of Dust and Disease.

In Westminster Hall, where the Lawyers convene,
These pestilent particles ever are seen :
Where wrangling and wrath can be hired with big
    fees,
You are sure of a market for Dust and Disease.

The Church should be free; but some heretics say
That at present the Vatican's in a bad way :
And some other Assemblies of learned D.D.'s
Are perhaps not exempted from Dust and Disease.

The Dissenters are thought a peculiar people,
More pious than those that sit under a Steeple :
But some one-sided views and intolerant pleas
Seem to savour a little of Dust and Disease.

But what of the Doctors? are *they* without flaw?
Is Medicine more pure than Religion or Law?
I suspect that some even with Doctors' degrees
Love to kick up a Dust and shake hands with Disease.

Diplomacy dresses her visage in smiles,
To conceal all the better her treacherous wiles:
But behind her false front a keen critic may seize
On strong proofs of her traffic with Dust and Disease.

Where Fashion and Luxury glitter like gold,
But where Beauty is bartered and Honour is sold,
Though the surface show little to shock or displease,
Yet beneath,—all is Misery, Dust, and Disease.

Some attacks on the lungs, that of woe would be full,
Are repelled by a filter of loose Cotton Wool:
But a barrier of brass, or a *chevaux-de-frise*,
Won't exclude some descriptions of Dust and Disease.

How long will these poison-germs stifle the day?
When will Truth's blessed light shed a purified ray?
When will Phœbus send heat, or Favonius a breeze,
To destroy or disperse all this Dust and Disease?

KEEP YOUR MOUTH SHUT.

[George Catlin, the friend and historian of the Red Races, produced ately a curious volume, published by Trübner & Co., entitled 'Shut your Mouth and Save your Life,' with illustrations. Mr Catlin here brings us a message from his Red friends, and an announcement that, with all our boasted civilisation, the unhealthy state of our population, and in particular, the high death-rate among our children and young persons, arise mainly from our disregard of a habit which universally prevails among the American Indians with the best results. The remedy for all our ailments, according to Mr Catlin, is simply that, waking and sleeping, but particularly when sleeping, we should, as much as possible, keep our mouth shut and breathe through our nostrils. This habit is early enforced by the Indian mother upon her children; and to this precaution is to be ascribed, as Mr Catlin alleges, the exemption of the Red race from those diseases which carry off so vast a proportion of our youthful population, and make so many of the rest of us the victims of lengthened bad health. By breathing through the mouth, he tells us, we pour in upon the lungs the unmodified and impure air of the ordinary atmosphere, to the destruction both of our breathing tubes and of the digestive apparatus of the mouth; while if we breathed through our nostrils, the air, in its progress through that passage, would be regulated in its temperature, and would be deprived of those deleterious particles which are diffused through it, and which are the great vehicles of infection. The nostrils, from their peculiar formation, are a natural respirator, better and safer than any artificial contrivance of that kind. In particular, Mr Catlin ascribes the epidemic decay of the dental organs which prevails nowadays so extensively among white men, to the action upon those parts of the improper mode of respiration in use. We attempt a versification of his theory.]

KEEP YOUR MOUTH SHUT.

H URRAH ! Old George Catlin has found out the cause
Why we've ailments, and aches, and bad teeth in our jaws :
No end of disorders will into you creep,
If you leave a door open while lying asleep :
But of most of life's ills you may make a clean cut,
If you breathe through your nostrils and keep your mouth shut.

His friends the Red tribes, men and squaws, boys and girls,
All have strong limbs and lungs, all have teeth pure as pearls ;
While We children of Europe are sickly and dying,
And have only good teeth of the dentist's supplying;
And the reason is this : In the Red Indian's hut,
They all breathe through their nostrils and keep their mouths shut.

The atmosphere's laden with Dust and Disease,
Coughs, Colds, and Consumptions, and worse, too, than
 these ;
And if atoms so noxious you swallow wholesale,
With the self-same result you might poison inhale :
But the nostrils, like filters, such ills will rebut ;
So make use of that passage and keep your mouth shut.

To renew life and strength, your night's sleep must be
 sound,
And your system well rested till morning comes round :
So old Catlin explains, what we all would explore,
How to sleep free from nightmare, with never a snore :
Let your head on a neat little pillow abut ;
Then breathe through your nostrils and keep your
 mouth shut.

A great gaping mouth mars the handsomest face,
For of wisdom and wit it destroys every trace ;
Even Beauty herself is less fair in our eyes,
With a wide open trap, as if set to catch flies ;
Mark the contrast in many a comic woodcut—
Which our author here gives—of mouths open and
 shut.

But Catlin's advice more instruction affords,
Than he thought of, perhaps, when he uttered his
    words :
He hoped he might lessen the Bills of Mortality,
But I think he may also improve our morality:
There are evils as serious as dust, smoke, or smut,
Where you'll find it a safeguard to keep your mouth
    shut.

When the banquet is spread, and the long-laboured
    feast
Still tempts you to eat when your hunger has ceased ;
When the wine-cup is bright, and you've basked in its
    ray,
Till you're conscious that prudence might quickly give
    way ;
Ere you venture still further your passions to glut,
Think of next morning's terrors, and keep your mouth
    shut.

When detraction and malice the absent assail,
And each speaker contributes a scandalous tale ;
If you can't use your tongue such attacks to arrest,
Let your silence at least be your solemn protest ;
Ere you brand friend or foe as a sot or a slut,
Think of Charity's mandates, and keep your mouth shut!

The Mouth, it appears, in the business of life,
Has two duties to do, yet they're seldom at strife:
In due season it needs to be open by day,
Any good thing to swallow, or good thing to say:
But at all other times, if you'd not be a butt
For disease or disaster, best keep your mouth shut !

GASTER, THE FIRST M.A.

" The ruler of this place was one Master Gaster, the first Master of Art in the world."—RABELAIS.

THERE'S a comical fellow that all of us know,
And who always is with us wherever we go ;
But our constant companion and guide though he be,
Yet out eyes never saw him, and never will see.
Of science the source, and of arts the first master,—
The name of this wonderful fellow is Gaster.

Search history through with attention and skill,
And you'll find him still busy for good or for ill.
With his mischievous doings you early may grapple
In the old and unhappy affair of the Apple.
Though the Serpent's designs mainly caused that disaster,
The Serpent was greatly assisted by Gaster.

But when Man was then sentenced to trouble and toil,
It was Gaster that taught him to labour the soil—
To dig and to delve, and to plant for his diet ;
And he never would let him a moment be quiet.

Despotic and stern, and a rigid taskmaster,
But an excellent friend and instructor, was Gaster.

After living some ages on water and greens,
Gaster found out that bacon ate nicely with beans;
And he also found out that, to moisten such food,
Something better than water was needful and good.
The Nymph of the Well owned that Bacchus surpassed
    her,
And gave way to the Grape as the liquor for Gaster.

Then baking, and brewing, and hunting, and fishing
Arose from what Gaster was wanting or wishing.
The grain in the furrow, the fruit on the tree,
The flocks on the mountains, the herds on the lee,
All acknowledged his sway; never empire was vaster
Than the fertile dominions thus subject to Gaster.

Geometry sprang from the Nile's spreading flood,
Just that Gaster might know where his landmarks had
    stood;
And Commerce grew busy by land and by sea,
Just that Gaster at home well-provisioned might be.
See! the camel, the car, the canoe, the three-master,
All speed with their loads on the missions of Gaster.

Then cities were built with their shops and their houses,
Where in plenty and peace Gaster feasts and carouses;
And a half of the houses and shops in a town,
If great Gaster were gone, might as well be pulled down:
So splendid and spacious on pier and pilaster
Rise the halls we've erected in honour of Gaster.

But I ought to observe that the changes thus made
For the most part took place with Dame Poverty's aid:
For Gaster and She, you don't need me to mention,
Are the father and mother of every invention.
When the pockets contain not a single piaster,
The wits become sharp in the service of Gaster.

I own we've had bloodshed by Gaster's advice,
And proceedings besides that were not over-nice.
Neither Rob Roy nor Cacus had been such a thief,
Hadn't Gaster been always so partial to beef.
When the Mosstrooper's wife saw he'd soon be a faster,
She served up his spurs at the bidding of Gaster.

Yet if Gaster would stay in his natural state,
His exactions would seldom be grievous or great.
But Luxury comes with suggestions officious,
And Cookery tempts him with dishes delicious,

And the Doctor's called in, with his rhubarb and castor,
To remove the sad ills of poor surfeited Gaster.

O ! close upon frenzy the maladies border
That Gaster begets when he's long out of order.
Like madmen we hurry, in hopes of release,
To Malvern or Homburg, to Gully or Spiess ;
When perhaps the disease would be put to flight faster,
If we just stayed at home and did justice to Gaster.

Try always to suit Gaster's wants to a tittle,
Nor supply his demands with too much or too little.
You will ne'er put a sick man in hearty condition,
If Gaster won't join and assist the physician.
In vain to a wound you'll apply salve or plaster,
If you don't take the pains to conciliate Gaster.

When Beauty puts forth all its glory and grace,
And unites the full splendour of form and of face ;
When each gesture is joyous, each movement is light,
And the glance of the eye is serene and yet bright ;
When the rose-hue of health tints the pure alabaster,—
Let us own that 'tis partly the doing of Gaster.

Nay, even in your noblest possession, the Mind,
Your dependence on Gaster too often you find.

A redundant repast, a rich supper or *soirée*,
Will oppress the *divinæ particulam auræ ;*
While at times, you may see, no professor or pastor
Teaches kindness and charity better than Gaster.

Oft when petty annoyances ruffle the soul,
And the temper defies philosophic control,
The commotion is quelled, and a calm will succeed,
Through the simple device of inhaling the Weed :
Such magical power has the soothing Canaster
To bring balmy content and good-humour to Gaster.

As for me, who thus venture his praise to proclaim,
And adorn his high worth with his classical name,
Let me hope from my patron these verses may bring
Some appropriate boon to assist me to sing ;
For it must be confessed that the poor poetaster
Finds always his best inspiration in Gaster.

October 1862.

NOTE.—If Gaster, as Rabelais says, was a Master of Arts, it seems a
precedent for Female Graduation, as Gaster in Greek is feminine.

GASTER.

(ADAPTED TO MUSIC.)

AIR—*The Rogue's March.*

I N a far distant age
  (*Vide* Rabelais' page)
Lived a fellow, of Arts the first Master:
  And if further you seek,
  I can tell you in Greek,
That the name of this fellow was Gaster.
  An ingenious fellow was Gaster,
  Though he caused us a little disaster:
  For if you'll look in,
  To our first parents' sin,
It was partly the greed of this Gaster.

  Thence into the world,
  Out of paradise hurled,
Adam found here a rigid taskmaster,

Who compelled him to work
Like a Trojan or Turk,
To provide a subsistence for Gaster :
O ! a terrible fellow was Gaster ;
Whose demands became vaster and vaster :
Man was destined to toil,
And to grub at the soil,
That there might be some grub to give Gaster.

When the infant first thought
How his milk could be brought
From its fountain of fair alabaster,
The nice milking machine
We so often have seen,
Was found out for the service of Gaster.
O ! Science must bend before Gaster,
Who in talent has often surpassed her :
Ere we knew what the cause
Of a Vacuum was,
It was made by a baby for Gaster.

Man, after the Flood,
Took to animal food,
As to which he had been a strict faster ;
And strong meat made him long
To have liquor as strong ;
So the grape was fermented for Gaster.

'Twas a perilous crisis for Gaster,
Who began after this to live faster :
  But provided he'd stop
  At a moderate drop,
It may prove a good cordial for Gaster.

And still, at this day,
Gaster figures away,
Our adviser, our guide, our schoolmaster;
  For the most things we do
  Have one object in view—
To provide a good dinner for Gaster.
  Trade and commerce are fostered by Gaster :
  The skiff, and the lofty three-master,
    Spread abroad their white sail
    To each varying gale,
  To bring victuals and drink here to Gaster.

But it makes me quite grave,
To think how we behave,
When we do not our appetites master;
  For we eat, and we swill,
  Twice as much as our fill,
Till we smother and suffocate Gaster.
  Then the doctor is sent for to Gaster,
Who prescribes for him rhubarb and castor ;

Gaster.

And so dose after dose
In and out of us goes,
To redress the distempers of Gaster.

A connection most rare
Bound the Siamese pair,
More completely than Pollux and Castor;
So the body and soul
Can each other control,
And the mind sympathises with Gaster.
A proper attention to Gaster
Saves many a potion and plaster:
Even Surgeons have found
That they can't heal a wound,
If they don't first propitiate Gaster.

Would you know the Chief Good
Men so much have pursued,
Since the era of old Zoroaster;
'Tis a conscience serene,
Hands and tongue that are clean,
And a healthy condition of Gaster.
Then fill up a bumper to Gaster:
Not forgetting the poor poetaster,
Who has lent you his time
For this doggerel rhyme,
As a small panegyric on Gaster.

F

BEEF AND POTATOES.

A DIETETIC DITTY.

AIR—*Potatoes grow in Limerick.*

" POTATOES grow in Limerick and beef in Bal-
limore;"
Use the two together, and of strength you'll have a store :
Beef supplies the fibre, while the *taties* feed the fire ;
And a little glass of good poteen will merriment inspire.

Every muscle as it moves some tear and wear sustains ;
And thus set free, the old debris find out their several
drains :
However sad the thought may seem, the fact is very
clear,
That day by day we waste away, and soon should dis-
appear.

But food is sent, with kind intent, the fabric to restore ;
The pot that boils our bit of beef rebuilds us as before ;

Or should we take, for England's sake, her roast beef so
   renowned,
You would not wish a nobler dish, with pudding duly
   browned.

A round of beef in winter time is found a joyous treat,
When pickled with a mixture where both salt and sugar
   meet ;
But salting needs correction, and Old Custom tells the
   means,
That the round should be encircled with a lively wreath
   of *greens.*

As some relief, when tired of beef, you'll find that mutton's good ;
With turnips and with caper-sauce, it makes a pleasant
   food :
Mutton old and claret good were Caledonia's forte,
Before the Southron taxed her drink and poisoned her
   with port.

If fowl or veal should be your meal, then have a slice of
   ham,
Where fat and lean, together seen, may save an extra
   dram :

But let your ham be duly boiled, and don't eat pork
  that's raw,
For fear that Trichiniasis should clutch you in its claw.

Some, *veluti in speculum*, survey their loss and gain,
And try by weight and measure nice a medium to maintain :
So when of all their goings-out they've found the just
  amount,
They eat, or starve, as best may serve to balance the
  account.*

But, sooth to say, a simpler way will do the job as well ;
Your appetite, if tight and right, will be your dinner-bell;
Eat whene'er you're hungry, and when hunger ceases—
  stop ;
And drink for love and friendship's sake a not immo-
  derate drop.

O happy he, from doctors free, who thus adjusts his fare,
As true and pat as if he sat in great Santorio's chair !
He doesn't take too little, and he doesn't take too much,
And a heart more sound will not be found, " from
  Canada to Cutch."

* See 'Spectator,' No. 25.

A SONG OF PROVERBS.

AIR—*Push about the jorum.*

IN ancient days, tradition says,
   When knowledge much was stinted—
When few could teach and fewer preach,
   And books were not yet printed—
What wise men thought, by prudence taught,
   They pithily expounded ;
And proverbs sage, from age to age,
   In every mouth abounded.

   O blessings on the men of yore,
      Who wisdom thus augmented,
   And left a store of easy lore
      For human use invented.

Two of a trade, 'twas early said,
   Do very ill agree, sir ;
A beggar hates at rich men's gates
   A beggar's face to see, sir.

Yet trades there are, though rather rare,
    Where men are not so jealous;
Two lawyers know the coal to blow,
    Just like a pair of bellows.
        O blessings, &c.

When tinkers try their trade to ply,
    They make more holes than mend, sir;
Set some astride a horse to ride,
    You know their latter end, sir.
Rogues meet their due when out they fall,
    And each the other blames, sir;
The pot should not the kettle call
    Opprobrious sorts of names, sir.
        O blessings, &c.

The man who would Charybdis shun,
    Must make a cautious movement,
Or else he'll into Scylla run—
    Which would be no improvement.
The fish that left the frying-pan,
    On feeling that desire, sir,
Took little by their change of plan,
    When floundering in the fire, sir.
        O blessings, &c.

A man of nous from a glass house
  Will not be throwing stones, sir;
A mountain may bring forth a mouse,
  With many throes and groans, sir.
A friend in need's a friend indeed,
  And prized as such should be, sir;
But summer friends, when summer ends,
  Are off and o'er the sea, sir.

  O blessings, &c.

Sour grapes, we cry, of things too high,
  Which gives our pride relief, sir;
Between two stools the bones of fools
  Are apt to come to grief, sir.
Truth, some folks tell, lies in a well,
  Though why I ne'er could see, sir;
But some opine 'tis found in wine :
  Which better pleases me, sir.

  O blessings, &c.

Your toil and pain will all be vain,
  To try to milk the bull, sir;
If forth you jog to shear the hog,
  You'll get more cry than wool, sir.
'Twould task your hand to sow the sand,
  Or shave a chin that's bare, sir;

You cannot strip a Highland hip
Of what it does not wear, sir.
    O blessings, &c.

I'm wae to think the Scottish tongue
    Is deein' oot sae fast, man ;
But some few sayin's may be sung
    Or e'er its day be past, man.
It's far o'er late the nest to seek,
    When a' the birds are flown, man ;
Or yet the stable-door to steek,
    When a' the steeds are stown, man.
    O blessings, &c.

Of proverbs in the common style
    If now you're growing weary,
I'll try again to raise a smile
    With two by Lord Dundreary.
You cannot brew good Burgundy
    Out of an old sow's ear, sir ;
Nor can you make a silken purse
    From very sour small beer, sir.
    O blessings, &c.

Now he who listens to my song,
    And heeds what I indite, sir,

Will seldom very far go wrong,
 And often will go right, sir.
But whoso hears with idle ears,
 And is no wiser made, sir,
A fool is he, and still would be,
 Though in a mortar brayed, sir.
  O blessings, &c.

January 1864.

A SONG OF TRUISMS.

AIR—*Vivan tutte.*

HARK to me, and I will tell you
Some things you may find of value :
Common-sense and useful knowledge
Are not only got at College.

This is true beyond a doubt,
Whosoever found it out.

Soldiers fight and fall in battle ;
Calves and cows are counted cattle ;
Sheep make turnips into mutton ;
Fat men's clothes don't freely button.

This is true, &c.

Oxygen combines with iron ;
Marvels great our lives environ ;
I've seen human bears and monkeys,
Plumeless geese and two-legged donkeys.

This is true, &c.

Ducks and Dutchmen love aquatics;
Some poor people live in attics;
Some set order at defiance;
Some believe in Social Science.

This is true, &c.

Wrinkles aren't cured by riches;
Some wives wear their husbands' breeches;
Beauties like to have their roses
Rather on their cheeks than noses.

This is true, &c.

Venison makes a noble pasty;
What is cheap is often nasty;
'Tis a project quite Utopian,
To wash white an Ethiopian.

This is true, &c.

If you wish to hear related
All the truths that could be stated,
I might thus go on till supper,
Near as wise as Martin Tupper.

This is true beyond a doubt,
But your patience now is out.

HOW TO MAKE A NOVEL.

AIR—*Bob and Joan.*

TRY with me and mix
    What will make a Novel,
All hearts to transfix
    In house or hall or hovel.
Put the caldron on,
    Set the bellows blowing,
We'll produce anon
    Something worth the showing.
      Toora-loora-loo, &c.

Never mind your *plot;*
    'Tisn't worth the trouble :
Throw into the pot
    What will boil and bubble.
Character's a jest ;
    What's the use of study ?

All will stand the test
  That's black enough and bloody.
    Toora-loora, &c.

Here's the 'Newgate Guide,'
Here's the 'Causes Célèbres;'
Tumble in beside,
  Pistol, gun, and sabre.
These Police reports
Those Old Bailey trials,
Horrors of all sorts,
  To match the Seven Vials.*
    Toora-loora, &c.

Down into a well,
  Lady, thrust your lover;
Truth, as some folks tell,
  There he may discover.
Stepdames, sure though slow,
  Rivals of your daughters,
Bring us from below
  Styx and all its waters.
    Toora-loora, &c.

---

* Seven Dials?—*Printer's Devil.*

Crime, that breaks all bounds,
  Bigamy and arson,
Poison, blood, and wounds,
  Will carry well the farce on.
Now it's just in shape;
  Yet, with fire and murder,
Treason, too, and rape
  Might help it all the further.

Toora-loora, &c.

.

Or, by way of change,
  In your wild narration
Choose adventures strange
  Of fraud and personation.
Make the job complete;
  Let your vile assassin
Rob and forge and cheat,
  For his victim passin'.

Toora-loora, &c.

Tame is Virtue's school;
  Paint, as more effective,
Villain, knave, and fool,
  With always a Detective.

Hate for Love may sit;
Gloom will do for Gladness,
Banish Sense and Wit,
And dash in lots of Madness.

Toora-loora, &c.

Stir the broth about;
Keep the furnace glowing :
Soon we'll pour it out
In three bright volumes flowing.
Some may jeer and jibe :
We know where the shop is,
Ready to subscribe
For a thousand copies !

Toora-loora-loo,
Toora-loora-leddy ;
Now the dish will do,
Now the Novel's ready.

HILLI-ONNEE.

[In the year 1841 Lord Palmerston had a celebrated race-horse called Ilione, the pronunciation of whose name became a matter of dispute on the turf. An appeal having been made to his lordship, he replied, to the surprise of some scholars, that it should be pronounced as if written Hillionnee. *Apparently this view arose from his lordship's having become a convert to the system of accentual pronunciation. The ordinary English mode of pronouncing the name is that indicated by Pitt in his translation of the Eneid, Book I., when he speaks of the sceptre*

" That wont Ilione's fair hand to grace."]

THE Whigs can boast of many a name,
　　Great Normanby and Little Johnny;
But far their foremost child of fame
Is he that owns fleet Hilli-onnee.

'Mong lords and legs a contest rose
　　As fierce as e'er was fought with Bonny:
From words, it almost came to blows,
And still the theme was Hilli-onnee.

And some said this and some said that;
　　No want there was of caco-phony:

With short and long, with sharp and flat,
    They sore misnomered Hilli-onnee.

Then One bethought him of a way
    To terminate this acri-mony ;
He called as umpire of the fray,
    The lord that owns fleet Hilli-onnee.

His lordship, though a scholar once,
    At this appeal was much *étonné;*
But loath to be esteemed a dunce,
    He searched his books for Hilli-onnee.

No doubt he well remembered yet
    Old Sophocles's *Hanti-gonnee;*
A clearer case he could not get,
    Nor more in point for Hilli-onnee.

But firmer proofs he sought and found ;
    The Greeks, disliking mono-tony,
Had accents to direct the sound,
    And these showed here 'twas Hilli-onnee.

He wrote his answer, brief, yet bright
    With classic wit and keen i-rony,

G

And having quashed the Tories quite,
He taught us all 'twas Hilli-onnee.

O Peel ! your guilt what tongue can tell !
'Twas nothing less than rank fe-lonny,
To oust a lord who talks so well
  Of heathen Greek and Hilli-onnee.

Had I the might of Pindar's muse
  To sing the praise of Palmer-stonny;
The deathless prince of Syracuse
  Should yield to him and Hilli-onnee.

Pindar, alas ! is in his grave ;
  But this good page of old E-bonny,
For distant days the name shall save
  Of Palmer-ston and Hilli-onnee.

November 1841.

THE TOURIST'S MATRIMONIAL GUIDE
THROUGH SCOTLAND.

A NEW SONG.

AIR— *Woo'd and married an' a'.*

YE tourists, who Scotland would enter,
   The summer or autumn to pass,
I'll tell you how far you may venture
   To flirt with your lad or your lass;
How close you may come upon marriage,
   Still keeping the wind of the law,
And not, by some foolish miscarriage,
   Get woo'd and married an' a'.

> *Woo'd and married an' a';*
> *Married and woo'd an' a':*
> *And not, by some foolish miscarriage,*
> *Get woo'd and married an' a'.*

This maxim itself might content ye,
    That marriage is made—by consent;
Provided it's done *de præsenti*,
    And marriage is really what's meant.
Suppose that young Jocky and Jenny
    Say, " We two are husband and wife ; "
The witnesses needn't be many—
    They're instantly buckled for life.

> *Woo'd and married an' a';*
> *Married and woo'd an' a':*
> *It isn't with us a hard thing*
> *To get woo'd and married an' a'.*

Suppose the man only has spoken,
    The woman just giving a nod ;
They're spliced by that very same token
    Till one of them's under the sod.
Though words would be bolder and blunter,
    The want of them isn't a flaw
For *nutu signisque loquuntur*
    Is good Consistorial Law.

> *Woo'd and married an' a';*
> *Married and woo'd an' a':*
> *A wink is as good as a word*
> *To get woo'd and married an' a'.*

If people are drunk or delirious,
  The marriage of course will be bad ;
Or if they're not sober and serious,
  But acting a play or charade.
It's bad if it's only a cover
  For cloaking a scandal or sin,
And talking a landlady over
  To let the folks lodge in her inn.

  Woo'd and married an' a';
  Married and woo'd an' a':
  It isn't the mere use of words
  Makes you woo'd and married an' a'.

You'd better keep clear of love-letters,
  Or write them with caution and care ;
For, faith, they may fasten your fetters,
  If wearing a conjugal air.
Unless you're a knowing old stager,
  'Tis here you'll most likely be lost ;
As a certain much-talked-about Major
  Had very near found to his cost.

  Woo'd and married an' a';
  Married and woo'd an' a':
  They are perilous things, pen and ink,
  To get woo'd and married an' a'.

I ought now to tell the unwary,
  That into the noose they'll be led,
By giving a promise to marry,
  And acting as if they were wed.
But if, when the promise you're plighting,
  To keep it you think you'd be loath,—
Just see that it isn't in writing,
  And then it must come to your oath.

Woo'd and married an' a';
Married and woo'd an' a':
I've shown you a dodge to avoid
Being woo'd and married an' a'.

A third way of tying the tether,
  Which sometimes may happen to suit,
Is living a good while together,
  And getting a married repute.
But you who are here as a stranger,
  And don't mean to stay with us long,
Are little exposed to that danger;
  So here I may finish my song.

Woo'd and married an' a';
Married and woo'd an' a':
You're taught now to seek or to shun
Being woo'd and married an' a'.

DECIMIS INCLUSI-S.

" Many lands in Scotland are enjoyed cum decimis inclusis et nunquam
antea separatis. *All our writers agree that such lands are free from the
payment of tithes."*—ERSKINE'S INSTITUTE.

AIR—*Maggie Lauder.*

I 'VE often wished it were my fate,
    Enriched by Fortune's bounty,
To own a little nice Estate
    In some delightful county ;
Where I, perhaps, with some applause,
    Might cultivate the Muses,
And till my lands, and have a clause
    Cum decimis inclusis.

Wherever no such clause appears,
    You're doomed to much vexation ;
The Minister, each twenty years,
    Pursues his augmentation.
Like any fiend he grabs your teind,
    Unless the Court refuses,

And all are sold who do not hold
Cum decimis inclusis.

That strife to tell, would answer well
This tune of Maggie Lauder,
When half the Bar are waging war
About the extra cha'der.
But Outram's * wit that scene has hit,
And all so much amuses,
That I refrain, and turn my strain
To *decimis inclusis.*

'Twould be a dry and dreary theme,
With nothing ornamental,
To tell you how the Interim scheme
Adopts the Proven rental ;
The Common agent in the suit,
Objecting where he chooses,
Is glad when he can well dispute
Your *decimis inclusis.*

A friend of mine had such a grant,
And did not get it *gratis;*
But when produced, 'twas found to want
The *nunquam separatis.*

* See Mr Outram's excellent song on the "Process of Augmentation."

An Heritor with such a flaw
  His whole exemption loses,
And might as well possess, in law,
  No *decimis inclusis.*

Then ere you buy, your titles try,
  For fear they're in disorder :
An Old Church feu's the thing for you,
  From some Cistercian Order.
Demand a progress stanch and tight,
  For nothing that excuses,
And see your *nunquam antea*'s right
  As well as your *inclusis.*

Then free from fear and free from strife,
  Your cares and troubles over,
You'll lead a gay and easy life
  Among your corn and clover.
The whole Teind Court you'll make your sport,
  Which else such awe diffuses,
" Augument away," you'll blithely say,
  " I've *decimis inclusis.*"

THE JOLLY TESTATOR WHO MAKES HIS OWN WILL.

AIR—*Argyll is my name.*

YE Lawyers who live upon litigants' fees,
   And who need a good many to live at your ease;
Grave or gay, wise or witty, whate'er your degree,
Plain stuff or Queen's Counsel, take counsel of me.
When a festive occasion your spirit unbends,
You should never forget the Profession's best friends;
So we'll send round the wine and a bright bumper fill
To the jolly Testator who makes his own Will.

He premises his wish and his purpose to save
All disputes among friends when he's laid in the grave;
Then he straightway proceeds more disputes to create
Than a long summer's day would give time to relate.
He writes and erases, he blunders and blots,
He produces such puzzles and Gordian knots,
That a lawyer, intending to frame the deed *ill*,
Couldn't match the Testator who makes his own Will.

Testators are good; but a feeling more tender
Springs up when I think of the feminine gender:
The Testatrix for me, who, like Telemaque's mother,
Unweaves at one time what she wove at another.
She bequeaths, she repeats, she recalls a donation,
And she ends by revoking her own revocation;
Still scribbling or scratching some new Codicil;
O! success to the Woman who makes her own Will.

'Tisn't easy to say, 'mid her varying vapours,
What scraps should be deemed Testamentary papers;
'Tisn't easy from these her intentions to find,
When, perhaps, she herself never knew her own mind.
Every step that we take, there arises fresh trouble:
Is the legacy lapsed? is it single or double?
No customer brings so much grist to the mill
As the wealthy old Woman who makes her own Will.

The Law decides questions of *meum* and *tuum*,
By kindly consenting to make the thing *suum*:
The Esopean fable instructively tells
What becomes of the oyster, and who get the shells.
The Legatees starve, but the Lawyers are fed;
The Seniors have riches, the Juniors have bread;
The available surplus, of course, will be Nil
From the worthy Testators who make their own Will.

You had better pay toll when you take to the road,
Than attempt by a byway to reach your abode ;
You had better employ a Conveyancer's hand,
Than encounter the risk that your will shouldn't stand.
From the broad beaten track when the traveller strays,
He may land in a bog, or be lost in a maze ;
And the Law, when defied, will revenge itself still
On the Man and the Woman who make their own Will.

O! HE WAS LANG O' COMING.*

AIR— *The Auld Wife ayont the fire.*

NED LOTHIAN took a work in hand,
To spread his fame throughout the land
And let the lieges understand
How learnèd was our Lothian.

But O ! he was lang o' coming ;
Very, very lang o' coming :
Surely he was lang o' coming ;
What could hinder Lothian ?

When Lothian did his plan arrange,
He looked for nothing new or strange :

---

* Mr Edward Lothian, an excellent lawyer and an excellent man, was
engaged in writing an Institute of the Law of Scotland ; but having kept
back his book for more than the Horatian period of gestation (it was
never published), a good many changes in the law took place, which,
with some anachronisms, are sought to be here represented. It should
be added that no one used to enjoy the singing of the song more than
the Subject of it.

But ere he finished—what a change !
How sore perplexed was Lothian !

But then he was sae lang o' coming, &c.

What powers the Admiral possessed,
And what with Commissaries rest—
Was all most learnedly expressed
In this great work by Lothian.

But why was he sae lang o' coming? &c.

How Services should be obtained
Before the Macers, he explained;
No part of this dark theme remained
Without some light from Lothian.

But then he was sae lang o' coming, &c.

The Admiralty Court is fled ;
The Commissaries—gone to bed ;
The Macers knocked upon the head ;
A heavy blow to Lothian !

But what made him sae lang o' coming? &c.

Election law he grappled fast ;
But when he held it at the last,

O! He was Lang o' Coming. 111

The Scotch Reform Bill had been passed ;
A fearful shock to Lothian !

But why was he sae lang o' coming? &c.

Of Sasines he had much to say;
But ere his chapter saw the day ;
Infeftments all were done away ;
 Another loss to Lothian !

But then he was sae lang o' coming, &c.

He wrote on Titles and Entails :
But little here his toil avails ;
For bit by bit the fabric fails,
 And nearly smothers Lothian.

But why sae very lang o' coming? &c.

In Teinds or Tithes he deep did search :
But these, too, left him in the lurch ;
The Liberals cashiered the Church,
 Just out of spite to Lothian.

But what made him sae lang o' coming? &c.

Yet still he worked 'gainst wind and weather,
Till Brougham one morning broke his tether,
Abolished Scotch Law altogether,
   And fairly finished Lothian.

But why was he sae lang o' coming?
Why sae very lang o' coming?
Surely he was lang o' coming;
   So good-night to Lothian!

SATURDAY AT E'EN.

Air—I gaed a waefu' gate yestreen.

COME all ye jolly lawyer lads who wrangle for a fee,
    Now lay aside your briefs a while, and sing this
    song with me:
For it's you, and you alone, can respond to what I mean,
And blithely raise the song in praise of Saturday at
    e'en.

    Of Saturday at e'en, boys, of Saturday at e'en;
    We'll blithely raise the song in praise of Satur-
       day at e'en.

Throughout the weary week we work, at morn, at noon,
    at night,
And spin our restless brains away to make the wrong
    seem right.
But our troubles and our toils they are all forgotten,
    clean,
When we broach a flask from Cockburn's cask on
    Saturday at e'en.

    On Saturday at e'en, &c.

H

To-night at last the married man enjoys his heart's
   desire,
And with his wife and children dear surrounds the
   cheerful fire;
While bachelors repair to some gay and glitt'ring scene,
Or court some bonnie lassie now on Saturday at e'en.
      On Saturday at e'en, &c.

Supremely blest among the rest, the Magnates on the
   Bench
Can smooth their brow and venture now their ardent
   thirst to quench :
Even the Junior on the Bills did not stand in awe of
   Skene,*
Nor fears to scan the face of Mann* on Saturday at e'en.
      On Saturday at e'en, &c.

But would you know where most I'd go these pleasant
   hours to pass;
With whom I'd wish to eat my fish, with whom to
   drink my glass?
It is not with the Advocate, it is not with the Dean,
But it's with some jolly junior boys on Saturday at e'en.
      On Saturday at e'en, &c.

* The names of well-known and excellent Bill-chamber Clerks.

Then come, ye jolly lawyer lads, another bottle draw,
Forget your condescendences, forget your pleas in law ;
If any state objections, we'll allow them to be seen,
But we'll meanwhile drain the cup again to Saturday
at e'en.

To Saturday at e'en, boys to Saturday at e'en ;
We'll meanwhile drain the cup again to Satur-
day at e'en.

THE SHERIFF'S LIFE AT SEA:

BEING PASSAGES IN THE LIFE OF A MARITIME SHERIFF.

[See Music in the Appendix.]

H OW gay is the Sheriff's roving life,
    Who from East to West can roam, boys:
How pleasant, with, or without, his wife,
  To sail for his Island home, boys. (*bis*)
      Roaming here,
      Foaming there,
      Merrily, cheerily,
      Readily, steadily;
Many an hour of mirth and glee
Has the Sheriff's life at sea, my boys.

When the steam is up and the goods are stored,
  And 'tis time to leave the Forth, boys,
The Sheriff gaily steps on board
  And steers away for the North, boys. (*bis*)

Steering here,
Veering there,
Merrily, cheerily,
Readily, steadily;
Quite from care and business free
Is the Sheriff's life at sea, my boys.

But the vessel breasts the eastern breeze,
  And St Andrews Bay is near, boys;
And the Sheriff tries to look at his ease,
  Though he feels a little queer, boys. (*bis*)
Pitching here,
Twitching there,
Cheerily, wearily, '
Ruefully, woefully;
Much inclined to make Dundee
Is the Sheriff now at sea, my boys.

Then the vessel nears to Aberdeen,
  And the plot is growing thick, boys:
On dinner bent the rest are seen,
  But the Sheriff's fairly sick, boys. (*bis*)
Cooking here,
Puking there,
Drearily, wearily,
Groaningly, moaningly;

Plain it is he don't agree
With a Sheriff's life at sea, my boys.

Yet afloat once more, when the waves are calm,
He tempts the treacherous main, boys ;
And the Sheriff cures the coming qualm
With a glass of good champagne, boys. (*bis*)
          Quaffing here,
          Laughing there,
          Cheerily, merrily,
          Readily, steadily ;
Quite intent upon a spree,
Is the Sheriff now at sea, my boys.

But the zephyr soon becomes a gale,
And the straining vessel groans, boys ;
And the Sheriff's face grows deadly pale,
As he thinks of Davy Jones, boys. (*bis*)
          Thinking here,
          Sinking there,
    `   Wearily, drearily,
          Shakingly, quakingly ;
Not from fear or sickness free
Is the Sheriff now at sea, my boys.

So the Sheriff here must needs resign,
For his inside's fairly gone, boys :

And he calls for a glass of brandy-wine,
,And to bed with his gaiters on, boys.   (*bis*)
   Lying here,
   Dying there,
  Drearily, wearily,
  Groaningly, moaningly;
 Prostrate laid by fate's decree
 Seems the Sheriff now at sea, my boys.

But a joyful strain awakes the Muse,
Which will quite efface the past, boys;
For the Mail-boat brings the joyful news
 That promotion's come at last, boys.   (*bis*)
   Cheering here,
   Jeering there,
  Merrily, cheerily,
  Readily, steadily:
 Fear and sickness far may flee,
 For the Sheriff quits the sea, my boys.

NOTE.—This song, describing the imaginary voyage of a Scotch Sheriff to his maritime dominions, was written as a parody on the song of " The Sailor's Life at Sea," which was one of the lyrics so delightfully sung by Professor Wilson. Another parody, in a different style, and by a different but certainly not an inferior hand, appeared in the Magazine under the title of " The Bagman's Life on Shore," May 1838.

LET US ALL BE UNHAPPY ON SUNDAY.

AIR—*We bipeds made up of frail clay.*

W E zealots, made up of stiff clay,
　　The sour-looking children of sorrow,
While not over-jolly to-day,
　　Resolve to be wretched to-morrow.
We can't for a certainty tell
　　What mirth may molest us on Monday;
But, at least, to begin the week well,
　　Let us all be unhappy on Sunday.

That day, the calm season of rest,
　　Shall come to us freezing and frigid;
A gloom all our thoughts shall invest,
　　Such as Calvin would call over-rigid.
With sermons from morning till night,
　　We'll strive to be decent and dreary:
To preachers a praise and delight,
　　Who ne'er think that sermons can weary.

All tradesmen cry up their own wares;
  In this they agree well together:
The Mason by stone and lime swears;
  The Tanner is always for leather.
The Smith still for iron would go;
  The Schoolmaster stands up for teaching;
And the Parson would have you to know,
  There's nothing on earth like his preaching.

The face of kind Nature is fair;
  But our system obscures its effulgence:
How sweet is a breath of fresh air!
  But our rules don't allow the indulgence.
These gardens, their walks and green bowers,
  Might be free to the poor man for one day;
But no, the glad plants and gay flowers
  Mustn't bloom or smell sweetly on Sunday.

What though a good precept we strain
  Till hateful and hurtful we make it!
What though, in thus pulling the rein,
  We may draw it so tight as to break it!
Abroad we forbid folks to roam,
  For fear they get social or frisky;
But of course they can sit still at home,
  And get dismally drunk upon whisky.

Then, though we can't certainly tell
How mirth may molest us on Monday;
At least, to begin the week well,
Let us all be unhappy on Sunday

THE THREE MODERATORS.

[*Written on the almost simultaneous appearance of three expositions of ecclesiastical views—the Addresses by the Moderators of the Established and Free Church Assemblies of Scotland, and an Allocution at Rome by the Pope on the State of the Catholic Church.*]

AIR—*Abraham Newland.*

W HEN a clerical set
In Assembly are met,
They are apt to prove angry debaters;
So, their wrath to restrain,
And due calmness maintain,
They have men that are called Moderators.
All Churches should have Moderators,
And should choose them of peaceable *naturs;*
Much trouble it saves
When some oil on the waves
Can be poured by your true Moderators.

But this good class of men,
I'm afraid, now and then,

To their office of peace have proved traitors ;
And too much, on the whole,
Have kept blowing the coal,
When they ought to have been Moderators.
What a pity that Church Moderators,
Like so many Vesuvian craters,
        Should send forth, in their ire,
        Thunder, fury, and fire
All around these inflamed Moderators.

        I took pains to compare
        The harangues from the chair
Lately made by two Reverend Paters ;
        And I read, the same day,
        What the Pope had to say—
For the Popes are just Rome's Moderators.*
The Pope and our two Moderators
Are surely not three Agitators !
        Yet it's clear that the *first*,
        Who, I hope, is the worst,
    Is no model for true Moderators.

        One famous divine,
        In his humorous line,

* The Pope and Cardinals, in their original constitution, may be said to
have been simply the Moderator and Presbytery of Rome, the Cardinals
being the supposed clergy of the City Churches.

Could not fail to delight all spectators ;
But some thought to his tongue
An astringency clung,
Scarcely known to our old Moderators.
The *third* of these same Moderators
I wish may have some imitators:
For Bisset to me,
Seemed the best of the three,
And comes nearest our true Moderators.

1862.

THE SONS OF THE MANSE.

A NEW SONG.

A<small>IR</small>—*This Brown Jug.*

O! LAW is a trade that's not easy to learn,
And a good many failures we daily discern;
But, touching this matter, I'm anxious to mention
A fact I've observed, that may claim some attention:
If you look round the Bar you will see at a glance
Not a few of the foremost are S<small>ONS</small> of the M<small>ANSE</small>.

Some glibly can *speak* what is not worth the speaking;
Some can *think*, but they still are for words vainly
 seeking;
A young man's best prospects will likely be blighted
If the tongue and the brains aren't duly united;
But if men who have *both* are here asked to advance,
You will find out that many are S<small>ONS</small> of the M<small>ANSE</small>.

In both Heads of the Court my assertion is proved,
For a Grandson is merely a Son once removed ;
Others' names I don't mention—the task would be
 tedious,
And perhaps might be found not a little invidious ;
But I often have witnessed a gay legal dance,
Where the whole four performers were SONS of the
 MANSE.

The Son of an Agent, his Son-in-law too,
May be certain at first to have something to do ;
Political friends may secure one a start—
Nay, a Clerk from an office may play a fair part :
But in time these will not have the ghost of a chance
With those dangerous rivals, the SONS of the MANSE.

I don't know how elsewhere these matters may be,
Though I daresay in England the like things they see ;
I remember at least that the race of the LAWS
Had both Bishops and Judges that met with applause ;
But in Italy, Spain, and in most parts of France,
They can scarce have *legitimate* SONS of the MANSE.

But talking of England, you'll keep it in view
That the Manse has sent thither a nursling or two :

Plain JOHN through high honours successfully passed,
And the Woolsack sustained his Fife "hurdies" at last ;
While BROUGHAM, in his pride, loved to caper and
    prance,
When, confessed, through his mother, a SON of the
    MANSE.

I don't mean to say that these shoots from the CHURCH
Have left all their brothers-in-law in the lurch ;
Good Sons of lay Sires, not a whit behind these,
Have their share of the talents, their share of the fees ;
But all parties will own that my song's no romance,
And that both Bench and Bar owe a debt to the MANSE.

Such wondrous results there's no way of explaining,
If we do not ascribe them to Clerical training;
The tyro begins with "the Chief End of Man,"
And "Effectual Calling" completes the great plan ;
Both Language and Logic his genius enhance,
Till he comes out a genuine SON of the MANSE.

Then here's to the MANSE ! both Established and Free,
And don't, I beseech you, leave out the U. P.;
SECEDERS good service performed in past years,
Though I'm sorry they call themselves now Volunteers ;

At the old Burgher Sect I can ne'er look askance,
When I think ROBERT JAMESON came from that MANSE.

I'm bound, too, I feel, on this joyous occasion,
To remember our Scottish Prelatic Persuasion;
And in justice, as well as with pleasure, to tell,
How our Law is indebted to GEORGE JOSEPH BELL;
Though their Church was held down and was weak in
    finance,
BELL, SANDFORD, and ALISON came from the MANSE.

The MANSE and the PULPIT, the BENCH and the BAR,
With the same godless enemies ever wage war;
They seek to subdue, by the pen, by the tongue,
DISSENSION, DISORDER, INJUSTICE, and WRONG.
How changed for the worse were broad Scotland's
    expanse,
If she hadn't the PARLIAMENT HOUSE—and the MANSE !

SONG SUNG AT THE SYMPOSIUM IN THE SALOON, 3D OF JANUARY 1840.

A TTEND to my song, ye contributors all,
   Now met to be merry in Ebony Hall:
Since justice has fully been done to the feast,
And the fury of hunger a moment has ceased,
Your hearts, I am sure, will allow it is fit
To drink, with due honours, a bumper to Kit !

A bumper to him, whose illustrious name
For ever must float on the full tide of fame :
While our little bark in attendance may sail,
Pursuing the triumph, and sharing the gale :
The fame will be ours on our tombs to have writ,
Here lies, who contributed something to Kit !

But while he is our head, and we're each but a limb,
He could do without us, though not we without him :
For were all his auxiliaries laid on the shelf,
He could knock off in no time a Number himself :

Let but steam and stenography help him a bit,
What tomes and what treasures might issue from Kit!

It is true he is old ; but 'tis easily seen,
Though his age may be gouty, it also is green :
He is garrulous, too, his detractors repeat;
But where was garrulity elsewhere so sweet?
Oh ! never did old age and eloquence sit
Half so comely on Nestor as now upon Kit !

And though thus resembling the Pylian Sire,
He has Ajax's force and Achilles's fire,
The softness that dwelt in Andromache's breast,
With the Ithacan's slyness to season the rest.
No wonder in Homer he made such a hit,
When Iliads and Odysseys centre in Kit !

The Crutch !—what a weapon in Christopher's hand !
The wind of its waving what force can withstand !
But his motto is noble, proclaim it aloud—
To spare the submissive and punish the proud :—
When his eye with benignity's beam is uplit,
What magic can equal the kindness of Kit !

Ere Christopher came a new era to bring,
The prose of the press was a pitiful thing :

There was hardness of heart, or else thickness of skull,
The witty were wicked, the worthy were dull:
The bright reconcilement of wisdom and wit—
To whom do we owe it?—entirely to Kit!

When riot and wrong seemed to rule in our isle,
And the boldest and best held their breath for a while,
Still true to his country and true to his creed,
Was Christopher found in the hour of our need:
When the ship on the breakers seemed ready to split,
The first boat to save her was manned by old Kit!

The times are much mended, but some things remain
That may call for the hand of the hero again:
For what with the Chartists, and what with the Church,
The law is of late rather left in the lurch.
Then his patriot rage may he never remit,
Till he floors every foeman of order and Kit!

Now may Christopher live, till in number we see
His years and his articles almost agree;
And may Maga's adherents, the high and the low,
Enjoy the best blessings her bounties bestow:
Even down to the *devils*, that never will quit,
But keep constantly howling for *copy* from Kit!

And here let our QUEEN put a close to my song—
May her life and her love both be happy and long !
A health to the youth whom her choice makes our own,
May her heart prove a dowry more rich than her
throne ;
And may all bad advisers be soon forced to flit,
And replaced by true subjects and sages like Kit !

SONG AT THE SYMPOSIUM ON MAGA.

AIR—*The Arethusa.*

COME, all good friends who stretch so free
Your legs beneath our Ebony,
In loving lays along with me,
    Proclaim the praise of Maga.
She is a creature not too good
For human nature's daily food :
    And her men are stanch to their favourite haunch,
    On which they fall like an avalanche,
    And fairly floor it, root and branch,
        In the name of mighty Maga.

'Tis sweet to see, when hard at work,
These heroes armed with knife and fork,
While flashes far the frequent cork
    To refresh the thirst of Maga.
Some dozen dishes swept away
Are but the prologue to our play :

If a haunch can't be found upon English ground,
Then the best of blackfaced, duly browned,
Or the faultless form of a well-fed round,
    Must sustain the strength of Maga.

Our banquet, lately spread to view,
Appears to me an emblem true
Of that served up in season due
    To the monthly guests of Maga.
No rival feast can e'er compare
With Maga's mental bill of fare,
    While her table is gay with a French fricassée,
    A currie, casserole, or a cabriolet,*
    Yet solid substance still bears sway
        In the rich repasts of Maga.

How many myriad mouths attend
Till Maga's hand their meat shall send!
What scholars, poets, patriots, bend
    Their eager eyes on Maga!
The knock that speaks a Number come,
Stirs the soldier's heart like the sound of a drum:
    While with pallid cheer, between hope and fear,
    Fair maidens ask, " Pray, does there appear

---

* A convenient name for any dish that has no other name.

Any more this month of Ten Thousand a-Year,
In the pleasing page of Maga?"

What fleets of Granton steamers sail,
Each laden with our monthly bale,
Besides that part that goes by rail,
  Of the wondrous works of Maga!
O'er all the earth, what scene or soil
Is not found full of Maga's toil?
  Every varying breeze wafts her over the seas,
  While insurance at Lloyd's is done with ease
  At nothing per cent, or what you please,
    On the craft that carries Maga.

Survey mankind with careful view,
From Cochin-China to Peru,
And take a transverse section too;
  All read and reverence Maga.
Around the poles, beneath the line,
She rules and reigns by right divine;
  She is thought no sin by Commissioner Lin;
  And, waiving at once the point of Pin,
  The Celestial Empire all take in
    The barbarian Mouth of Maga.

But most her page can joy impart
To many a home-sick Scottish heart,
That owns afar the potent art
Possessed by mighty Maga.
The exile sees, at her command,
His native mountains round him stand;
In vision clear his home is near,
And a murmuring streamlet fills his ear;
Till now the fast o'erflowing tear
Dissolves the spell of Maga.

But next let North inspire the strain:
Ye Muses, ope your richest vein!
Though flattery goes against the grain
With the master-mind of Maga.
Without him all to wreck would run:
A system then without a sun!
For his eye and soul, with strong control,
Enlighten all that round him roll,
And gild and guide the mighty whole,
That bears the name of Maga.

Then, now before we bid adieu,
We wish, while yet the year is new,

Succeeding seasons, not a few,
  To the noble North and Maga.
May life's best gifts their progress bless !
May their lights—and their shadows—never be less !
  May they lengthen their lease with an endless increase!
  Or only then depart in peace,
  When frauds shall fail and follies cease,
    Subdued by North and Maga.

February 1841.

HEY FOR SOCIAL SCIENCE, O!

A SONG FOR THE SOCIAL SCIENCE MEETING
AT GLASGOW IN 1860.

AIR—*Green grow the rashes, O!*

A PLEASANT week I lately passed
In Glasgow town,—no, city, O!
With men of state and merchants great,
And sages wise or witty, O!

CHORUS—*Hey for Social Science, O!*
Hey for Social Science, O!
When wisdom, wine, and wit combine,
They make a good alliance, O!

We met to show that all below
To ruin fast is tending, O!
That laws and schools and prison rules
Are much in need of mending, O!

Hey for Social Science, &c.

But though, no doubt, 'twas well made out
    That things are old and wheezy, O !
O cursed spite ! to set them right
    Was not so very easy, O !

Hey for Social Science, &c.

Yet though the task may patience ask,
    We're here convened to try it, O !
To see if schools will root out fools,
    Or crime be cured by diet, O !

Hey for Social Science, &c.

The blood-red sun had scarce begun
    To shine out strong and hearty, O !
When up we rose and donned our clo'es
    To join Bell's breakfast-party, O !

Hey for Social Science, &c.

Delicious doles of meat and rolls
    Disposed to mirth and laughter, O !
The inspiring tea brought out Macnee,
    And others followed after, O !

Hey for Social Science, &c.

When hunger's rage we thus assuage,
    Succeeds the thirst for knowledge, O !

Then, horse and foot, we take the *route*,
And hurry to the College, O !
  Hey for Social Science, &c.

Here in we press for some Address
  That lasts two hours or longer, O !
And if a word is seldom heard,
  The applause is all the stronger, O !
  Hey for Social Science, &c.

The Section Meetings next we try,
  Some worse and others better, O !
But if the days are somewhat dry,
  The nights will prove the wetter, O !
  Hey for Social Science, &c.

That sense alone conspicuous shone
  I can't declare in conscience, O !
But great's the use to introduce
  A safety-valve for nonsense, O !
  Hey for Social Science, &c.

A few who well their tale could tell
  Did ably fill the rostrums, O !

While many a goose his clack let loose,
And quacks proclaimed their nostrums, O !

Hey for Social Science, &c.

Just ere the welcome hour of six
We gladly cut our cable, O !
And in some port of refuge fix,
Hard by a well-spread table, O !

Hey for Social Science, &c.

While all things good in drink and food
Our weary souls are cheering, O !
The ills of life, before so rife,
Seem quickly disappearing, O !

Hey for Social Science, &c.

Around us eyes and faces bright
Our softened hearts are winning, O !
Fair matrons in meridian light,
And morning stars beginning, O !

Hey for Social Science, O !
The best of Social Science, O !
Is when its power, in hall or bower,
To Beauty we affiance, O !

With ardour fired, by love inspired,
  I rise and give " The Ladies," O !
And they who shrink the toast to drink
  May hang and go to Hades, O !

  Hey for Social Science, &c.

We talk, we quaff, we sing and laugh,
  Then part with tears and sighing, O !
And when at last the week is past
  We're dead with mirth—or dying, O !

  Hey for Social Science, &c.

But I ordain that soon again,
  These pleasant hours repeating, O !
We learn some more of Social lore
  At such an evening meeting, O !

  Hey for Social Science, O !
  For genuine Social Science, O !
  A summons here to recompear
  Would find a quick compliance, O !

I'M VERY FOND OF WATER.

A NEW TEMPERANCE SONG.

"Affirming that for constant use there was no liquor like a cup of English water, provided it had malt enough in it."—Addison's Freeholder.

Ἄριστον μὲν ὕδωρ.

[See Music in the Appendix.]

I'M very fond of water,
   I drink it noon and night:
Not Rechab's son or daughter
Had therein more delight.

I breakfast on it daily;
   And nectar it doth seem,
When once I've mixed it gaily
   With sugar and with cream.
But I forgot to mention
   That in it first I see,
Infused or in suspension,
   Good Mocha or Bohea.

CHORUS—*I'm very fond of water,*
 I drink it noon and night :
 No mother's son or daughter
 Hath therein more delight.

At luncheon, too, I drink it,
 And strength it seems to bring :
When really good, I think it
 A liquor for a king.
But I forgot to mention—
 'Tis best to be sincere—
I use an old invention
 That makes it into Beer.

   CHORUS—*I'm very fond of water,* &c.

I drink it, too, at dinner ;
 I quaff it full and free,
And find, as I'm a sinner,
 It does not disagree.
But I forgot to mention—
 As thus I drink and dine,
To obviate distension,
 I join some Sherry wine.

   CHORUS—*I'm very fond of water,* &c.

K

And then when dinner's over,
　And business far away,
I feel myself in clover,
　And sip my *eau sucrée*.
But I forgot to mention—
　To give the glass a smack,
I add, with due attention,
　Glenlivet or Cognac.

　　　CHORUS—*I'm very fond of water*, &c.

At last when evening closes,
　With something nice to eat,
The best of sleeping doses
　In water still I meet.
But I forgot to mention—
　I think it not a sin
To cheer the day's declension,
　By pouring in some Gin.

CHORUS—*I'm very fond of water :*
　It ever must delight
　Each mother's son or daughter—
　When qualified aright.

June 1861.

THE PERMISSIVE BILL.

A NEW SONG.

[See Music in the Appendix.]

" PRAY, what is this Permissive Bill,
    That some folks rave about?
I can't, with all my pains and skill,
    Its meaning quite make out."
O ! it's a little simple Bill,
    That seeks to pass *incog.*,
To *permit* ME—to *prevent* YOU—
    From having a glass of grog.

    Yes! it's a little simple Bill, &c.

If I'm a Quaker sly and dry,
    Or Presbyterian sour;
And look on all, with jaundiced eye,
    Who love a joyous hour:

O ! here I've my Permissive Bill,
  You naughty boys to flog,
And *permit* ME—to *prevent* YOU—
  From having a glass of grog.

  O ! yes, I have my little Bill, &c.

If I have wealth or means enough
  To import a pipe of wine;
While You a glass of humbler stuff
  Must purchase when you dine :
O ! then I use my little Bill,
  While wetting well my prog,
To *permit* ME—to *prevent* YOU—
  From buying a glass of grog.

  O ! yes, I use my little Bill, &c.

If I'm a fogie quite used up,
  And laid upon the shelf;
Who grudge that You still dine and sup,
  As I was wont myself:
Then I bring out my pretty Bill,
  To impose a little clog,
And *permit* ME—to *prevent* YOU—
  From having a glass of grog.   .

  Yes, I bring out my pretty Bill, &c.

If You can drink a sober drop,
  While I the bottle drain ;
And as I don't know when to stop,
  I'm ordered to "abstain :"
O ! then I've my Permissive Bill,
  Since I'm a drunken dog,
To *permit* ME—to *prevent* YOU—
  Enjoying a glass of grog.

     O ! yes, I've my Permissive Bill, &c.

" However well a man behaves,
  Life's pleasures must he lose,
Because a lot of fools or knaves
  Dislike them, or abuse ? "
O ! yes, and soon a bigger Bill,
  Will go the total hog,
And *permit* ME—to *prevent* YOU—
  Having Mirth as well as Grog.

CHORUS—*O ! yes, a big Permissive Bill,*
     Will go the total hog,
     And permit ME—*to* prevent YOU—
     Having Liberty, Mirth, or Grog.

June 1866.

OLD NOAH'S INVENTION.

AIR—*Miss Julia.*

WE read that old Noah, soon after the Flood,
  Found out a new liquor to quicken his blood :
Of water grown tired in his long navigation,
He hit on the process of vinification.
It doesn't appear that he took out a patent,
But the wondrous discovery wasn't long latent ;
For Noah, though such might not be his intention,
Got drunk on this very stupendous invention.

And ever since then we have evidence ample,
Mankind have been following Noah's example.
Sometimes they get drunk, and sometimes they do not;
But the business of drinking is seldom forgot.
They drink when they're merry, they drink when they're
    sad ;
They drink whensoever good drink's to be had.

What marriage or christening would meet with attention,
If you didn't still practise this wondrous invention?

The Wine-Cup may Poetry claim as a daughter,
Though a poet or two have been drinkers of water :
Good wine to the wise is a swift-wingèd steed,
While abstainers in general come little speed.
Would Homer or Horace have written a line,
Without plenty of Greek and Falernian wine?
What where North without Ambrose? or who would
e'er mention
A Socratic repast without Noah's invention?

Old Plato, the prince of political sages,
For the uses of drinking his credit engages.
When pleasure invites, if you'd learn self-denial,
A convivial meeting will serve as a trial.
Should you wish to find out if a man's a good fellow,
His virtues and faults will appear when he's mellow :
To whatever good gifts he may e'er make pretension,
The truth you can test by old Noah's invention.

Some folks would persuade us from drink to abstain,
For they trace ev'ry crime to that terrible bane:

But if drinking's a sin, yet I cannot help thinking,
Mankind have had sins independent of drinking.
The Antediluvians were free from that curse;
But their lives were no better,—in fact, they were
  worse:
And at least you can't prove any moral declension,
Since the date when old Noah made known his
  invention.

Then wisely partake of the generous juice;
But don't forfeit the boon by excess or abuse.
At your board let the Muses and Graces be found,
And the light-hearted Virtues still hover around.
And let this, I beseech you, be one of your rules,
Never show any folly in presence of fools;
For the wise man alone has a due comprehension,
And can make a right use—of old Noah's invention.

THE PLANTING OF THE VINE.

A RABBINICAL LEGEND.

AIR—*The Year that's awa'.*

WHEN Noah first planted the Vine,
    The Devil contrived to be there,
For he saw pretty well that the Finding of Wine
    Was a very important affair.

Mankind had been sober before;
    But had *not* been remarkably good;
And the cold-blooded crew had deserved all the more
    To be deluged and drenched by the Flood.

To assist us in mending our ways,
    And more safely our time to employ,
It was kindly determined to shorten our days,
    And afford us some generous joy.

l

Then the grape came to gladden man's heart;
  And a bright dawn of bliss seemed to glow,
When the rainbow and wine-cup could tidings impart,
  Of an end both to Water and Woe.

So to hallow the newly-found fruit,
  Noah chose a white Lamb without spot;
And he poured its young blood round the delicate root,
  To preserve it from blemish and blot.

But the Devil, such bounty to clog,
  And to substitute evil for good,
Slaughtered also a Lion, an Ape, and a Hog,
  And manured the young plant with their blood.

The first gush of the Vine's precious balm
  Shows its power in an innocent way:
Like the Lamb's gentle nature, our temper is calm,
  While our spirits are playful and gay.

But on tasting more freely the cup,
  Then its Leonine vices are found;
With a combative ardour the heart is lit up,
  And resentment and wrath hover round.

Next, the Ape, if still deeper we drink,
  His grimaces and gambols will try;
Till at last, like the Hog, oversated we sink,
  And contented lie down in the sty.

In avoiding these villainous beasts,
  Let our sense of the blessing be shown :
Let the Lamb's playful spirit preside at our feasts,
  Nor let even the Lion be known.

But I would not be ruthlessly told
  From all temperate draughts to refrain;
Lest perhaps, like the sober transgressors of old,
  We should bring down the Deluge again.

A BOTTLE AND FRIEND.

[See Music in the Appendix.]

WHEN the evening of life comes with temperate
ray,
To cool the hot blood that has boiled all the day;
When our faculties flag, and our frolics are o'er,
And our favourite idols are worshipped no more;
May some sober pleasures that season attend,
And Fortune still leave us—a Bottle and Friend.

When Beauty grows shy, and don't think it worth while
On an agèd admirer to lavish a smile:
When we, too, are backward, where oft we were bold,
And we don't fall in love once a-week as of old;
As some compensation, may Providence send,
To warm our cold bosoms—a Bottle and Friend.

When even Ambition has ceased to ensnare,
And we're calmly content to remain what we are:

When the Passions die out, of their fuel bereft,
And Ill-nature and Avarice only are left;
From Age and its evils our breasts to defend,
You'll find the best buckler—a Bottle and Friend.

Philosophers say, that the most of mankind,
In the things that they pray for, are foolish and blind;
That what seems a blessing oft turns out a bane,
And that Pleasure is merely the prelude to Pain:
But thus far our wishes may surely extend,
That there ne'er may be wanting—a Bottle and Friend.

A FLASK OF ROSY WINE.

A SEMI-SCIENTIFIC SONG.

[See Music in the Appendix.]

TO make life's pulses gaily go,
  Not much too fast, nor yet too slow ;
And joy without dejection know,
  Were worth a golden mine.
Then try with me the simple art,—
If better views you can't impart,—
To calm the brain and cheer the heart
  With a flask of rosy Wine.

Cognac may better suit with some,
Or Gin and Whisky handier come ;
And Glasgow long was fond of Rum
  When merchants met to dine :
But prudence there her part should play,
The fire with water to allay ;
Or take instead, to wet her clay,
  A flask of rosy Wine.

The rustic loves a rousing bout
With home-brewed Ale or bottled Stout :
When these are in the sense is out,
    And wit shows little sign.
For dull and dense *his* thoughts appear
That's drinking and that's thinking beer :
There's nothing keeps the head so clear
    As a flask of rosy Wine.

The Poppy's gifts can pain control,
And waft on wings the ravished soul,
While dreamy visions round us roll,
    Where rainbow-hues combine :
But sad reaction comes at last,
And binds the helpless victim fast :
Such gloomy shadows ne'er o'ercast
    The reign of rosy Wine.

The Hemp,—with which we used to hang
Our prison pets, yon felon gang,—
In Eastern climes produces Bang,
    Esteemed a drug divine.
As Hashish dressed, its magic powers
Can lap us in Elysian bowers;
But sweeter far our social hours
    O'er a flask of rosy Wine.

The Tartar's steeds, alive or dead,
Their master keep refreshed and fed ;
The steaks they yield, like saddles spread,
      Are cooked beneath his spine :
The milky mothers of his stud,
Outdoing those that chew the cud,
With Koumiss stir his stagnant blood,
      As if with rosy Wine.

The Indian race of famed Peru,
To mash their malt the Chica chew ;
And Tonga's tribes the same way brew
      What serves their Royal line.
The Court collects at dawn of day,
And munching sits and spits away :
The Monarch drinks ; but, sooth to say,
      It is not rosy Wine !

A Fungus, on Siberia's plain,
The toper's zeal can so sustain,
That he passes the bottle again and again,
      And gets drunk on the filtered brine.
Our liquor is not quite so strong,
And won't so well the war prolong ;
But much the fitter theme for song
      Is our flask of rosy Wine.

Folks up and down will preaching run
That Man should all such influence shun :
They might as well forbid the Sun
    In heaven at noon to shine.
We needs must seek, while here below,
Some kind Nepenthé for our woe ;
And what can softer balm bestow
    Than a flask of rosy Wine ?

The banquet is not spread in vain,
Nor instincts given to cause us pain ;
Yet Reason's hand should hold the rein,
    And Taste our joys refine :
And trust me, friends, for temperate use
Those vine-clad hills their sweets produce,
And Nature's self exalts the juice
    That fills our flask with Wine.

A PAGE OR TWO OF EPIGRAMS, &c.

THE BEST MEDICAL ATTENDANTS.

With Doctor Diet, and Doctor Quiet,
And now and then good Doctor Merryman,
Disease—you almost may defy it,
And cheat for years the Stygian ferryman.

ON WRITING ONE'S OWN EPITAPH.

Write your own epitáph in high-flown phrases;
Extol your merits with the loudest praises;
Paint every virtue in the brightest hue;
Then—*live a life* that shall approve it true.

FRENCH AND ENGLISH.

The French excel us very much in millinery;
They also bear the bell in matters culinary.
The reason's plain: French beauty and French meat,
With English cannot of themselves compete.
Thus, an inferior article possessing,
Our neighbours help it by superior dressing.
They dress their dishes, and they dress their dames,
Till Art, almost, can rival Nature's claims.

ANSWER BY HENRY ERSKINE TO THE DUCHESS OF GOR-
DON, WHO REFUSED TO GO TO A COUNTY BALL AS
IT WOULD BE "VULGAR AND DULL."

(*Versified.*)

"Vulgar and dull;" you'll therefore stay away?
That is, methinks, as if the Sun should say
"A dark, cold morning: I'll not rise to-day;"
Forgetting that the source of heat and light
Makes by its presence all things warm and bright.

INSCRIPTION ON A PLACARD PLACED NEAR THE CUS-
TOMARY SEAT OF A BLIND BEGGAR IN THE STREETS
OF PARIS.

(*Translated.*)

Good passers-by, for Jesus' sake,
Let this poor man your alms partake;
The blind recipient will not know
From whom such pious bounties flow;
But God, the All-seeing, will regard them,
And richly, as I pray, reward them.

THE TUFT-HUNTER.

After O'Dowd.

They call me a Tuft-hunter; but I say the TUFT hunts
me,
And in the mutual league we've made, I'm needed more
than he.
He finds the wine, I find the wit, the guests are well
requited;
But his *good things*, apart from mine, would little have
delighted.
I bring it to this issue, and there cannot be a plainer:
At last night's feast, should he or I, be called the
Entertainer?

A LATIN RECIPE FOR FRAMING AN INDICTMENT.

For the Use of Advocates-Depute.

Quando, ubi, quo pacto, quis, quid, patraverit, in quem,
Rectè compositus quisque libellus habet.

(Translation.)

A good Indictment, if you follow Hume,
Shows When, Where, How, Who, did What wrong, to
Whom.

L'Envoy.

I SEE how other men aspire,
   Who lofty strains can nobly raise ;
And feel that this, my humble lyre,
   Must yield to them the meed of praise.

But Mirth may come to Virtue's aid,
   When gloom the face of day would hide ;
And Truth, in mirthful garb arrayed,
   May find an entrance, else denied.

Then scorn not thou the sportive lay,
   Nor judge it by the rigid letter ;
With covert aim it winds its way
   By smiling paths to make men better.

On reading after a long interval the parody on "The Sailor's Life at Sea," referred to in our Note on p. 119, it appears to us so good that we cannot help adding it as a *pendant* to our own attempt.   It was written by a dear friend and frequent *collaborateur* of the present writer's.

.

THE BAGMAN'S LIFE ON SHORE.

AIR—*The Sailor's Life at Sea.*

H OW gay is the Bagman's bustling life,
Who from east to west can roam, sir !
In every town he finds a wife,
In every inn a home, sir.
Courting here,
Sporting there,
Merrily, readily,
Cheerily, steadily;
Many a joyous hour in store
Has the Bagman's life on shore.

With his three-caped coat and buckskins tight,
And the crape around his beaver,

And his mourning breast-pin full in sight,
  He looks a gay deceiver.
        Leering here,
        Jeering there,
        Merrily, readily,
        Cheerily, steadily,
    Hearts he conquers by the score;
    Such the Bagman's life on shore.

When cash grows low and the bill runs high,
  And the landlady looks amiss, sir,
The Bagman tips her a wink of his eye,
  And he pays his way with a kiss, sir.
        Smirking here,
        Shirking there,
        Merrily, readily,
        Cheerily, steadily,
    Till his gig is at the door;
    Such the Bagman's life on shore.

When the gig draws up and the bags are stored,
  And the bill has thus been paid, sir,
The Bagman lightly skips on board,
  With a " Damme, who's afraid, sir?"

Swearing here,
Staring there,
Merrily, readily,
Cheerily, steadily,
Care and thought he votes a bore;
Such the Bagman's life on shore.

At each toll-bar he can cheer his heart
With a cup of old October;
For he knows that a Bagman drunk may start,
While his horse and gig are sober.
Singing here,
Swinging there,
Merrily, readily,
Far from steadily;
Safe, though tempests round him roar,
Is the Bagman's course on shore.

When the storm is past, and the journey done,
And the tumbler smokes before him,
He cheers each waiter with his fun,
And the barmaids all adore him.
Funning here,
Punning there,

Merrily, readily,
Cheerily, steadily;
Tumblers three, or rather four,
Are the Bagman's rule on shore.

When the Bagman closes at last his books,
And stops at the sign of the Tomb, sir;
He meets the waiter with cheerful looks,
That shows him to his room, sir.
Jesting here,·
Resting there,
Wearily, readily,
Cheerily, steadily;
Soundest sleep, without a snore,
Be the Bagman's rest on shore.

Unconsciously, perhaps, the author of this song has in the last verse
indulged in a jest to be found in Milton's lines "On the University Carrier"
—the only jest perhaps that Milton ever perpetrated—where he tells of
Hobson, as at the end of his journey, and come to "his latest inn," that
Death—
          " In the kind office of a *chamberlin*,
     Showed him his room, where he must lodge that night,
     Pulled off his boots, and took away the light."

APPENDIX.

MUSIC OF SOME OF THE PRECEDING SONGS.

Original or Adapted.

THE LEATHER BOTTÈL.

See Chappell's *Popular Music of the Olden Time,* vol. ii. 513.

How ma - ny wond-rous things there be Of

which we can't the rea - son see! And this is one, I

used to think, That most men like a drop of drink. But

here comes Darwin with his plan, And shows the true De-

scent of Man: And that explains it all full well, For

man — was — once —— a leather bot - tèl!

THE SHERIFF'S LIFE AT SEA.

How gay is the Sher - iff's rov - ing life, Who from

East to West can roam, boys: How pleas-ant, with, or with -

bis.

| 1st time. | 2d time. |

- out, his wife, To sail for his Is - land home, boys.

Roam - ing here, Foam-ing there, Mer - ri - ly, cheer - i - ly,

Read - i - ly, stead - i - ly; Man - y an hour of

mirth and glee Has the Sher - iff's life at sea, my boys.

I'M VERY FOND OF WATER.

I'm ver - y fond of wa - ter, I drink it

noon and night: Not Re - chab's son or daugh - ter Had

there - in more de - light. I break - fast on it dai - ly;

And nec - tar it doth seem, When once I've mix'd it

gai - ly With su - gar and with cream. But I for -

- got to men - tion That in it first I see, In -

- fused or in sus - pen - sion, Good Mo - cha or Bo - hea.

THE PERMISSIVE BILL.

"Pray, what is this Per - mis - sive Bill, That some folks

rave a - bout? I can't, with all my pains and skill, Its

mean - ing quite make out." O! it's a lit - tle

sim - ple Bill, That seeks to pass *in - cog.*, To *per -*

mit ME to *pre - vent* YOU from hav - ing a glass of grog.

A BOTTLE AND FRIEND.

When the even - ing of life comes with tem - per - ate ray, To

cool the hot blood that has boil'd all the day ; When our

fac - ul - ties flag, and our fro - lics are o'er, And our

fav - our - ite i - dols are wor-shipp'd no more ; May some so - ber

plea-sures that sea - son at - tend, And Fortune still leave us — a

Bot - tle and Friend, A Bot - tle and Friend, A Bot - tle and

Friend, And For - tune still leave us — a Bot - tle and Friend.

A FLASK OF ROSY WINE.

To make life's pul - ses gai - ly go, Not much too fast, nor

yet too slow; And joy with - out de - jec - tion know, Were

worth a gold - en mine. Then try with me the sim - ple

art, If bet - ter views you can't im - part, To calm the

brain and cheer the heart, With a flask of ros - y Wine.

www.ingramcontent.com/pod-product-compliance
Lightning Source LLC
Chambersburg PA
CBHW022357020726
47500CB00002B/314